JESSIE'S GIFT

Jessie's Gift

Helen Brooks Regan

This memoir is a blend of real life and fiction. Some of the names, characters, businesses, places, events, and incidents may be real while other elements may have been fictionalized to enhance the narrative.

ISBN 978-1-62806-455-1 (paperback)

Library of Congress Control Number 2025911783

Published by Salt Water Media
29 Broad Street, Suite 104
Berlin, MD 21811
www.saltwatermedia.com

Cover images are courtesy of the author.

Interior images are courtesy of the author, in the public domain, or are used with permission from the owner.

Table Of Contents

Part II — Woo and Me: 1945 - 1987

Preface

> But what is the point of writing if not to unearth things, or even just one thing that cannot be reduced to any kind of psychological or sociological explanation, and is not the result of a preconceived idea or demonstration, but a narrative: something that emerges from the creases, where a story is unfolded, and can help us understand—endure—events that occur, and the things that we do?
>
> — Annie Ernaux
> *A Girl's Story*

This story is a tribute to my maternal grandparents, Jessie Townsend Lewis (1892-1987), and Milton Parks Lewis (1898-1962), for their profound influence on my life. I loved them both deeply, but because my grandfather died when I was just seventeen, but my grandmother lived until I was forty-two and she was ninety-five, this is primarily her story.

Raised by a cold and distant mother, and almost crushed by a relentless series of losses extending from childhood into adulthood, my grandmother developed effective emotional defenses which simultaneously equipped her to persevere in the face of tragedy and impaired her ability to establish intimate relationships. Inadvertently, I am sure, she transmitted the consequences of loss into the succeeding generation by raising my mother in the same cold and distant manner with which her mother had raised her. However, for some unknown reason, with the fourth generation she let down her emotional defenses, allowing love for her grandchildren to bloom.

We grandchildren called our grandparents WooWoo and Papoo. Family lore has it that I, the firstborn, was coached to call my paternal grandmother Lulu, which was her name, but I had trouble with Ls as I learned to talk. Perhaps I transposed *Lulu* into *WooWoo,* which became my generic toddler word for grandmothers. Perhaps I then transposed *Papa* for grandfather into the satisfying rhyming word *Papoo.* No one really knows. In any case, these names stuck. My younger sisters accepted them without question. When I was a teenager, I went for expediency and dropped one of WooWoo's Woos; my sisters immediately followed suit.

I have many memories of both my grandparents, some based on personal experiences with them, but, in my grandmother's case especially, also based on the stories she told me and my sisters when we were children. She was a mesmerizing storyteller, and we begged for stories each time we saw her. As a result, I heard the stories many times, and they are seared into my brain. I began my project to honor her by recording some of these stories; they form the early chapters.

Because Woo's stories did not span the full arc of her life, I needed to supplement them with information from newspapers of the day. *The Democratic Messenger,* the newspaper of Snow Hill, Maryland, her birthplace and childhood home, is now fully digitized online. For information about her adult life after she married my grandfather and moved to Wilmington, Delaware, where both my mother and I were born, I turned to *The Wilmington News-Journal*, also digitized online. Additionally, I did online research on pertinent topics such as pharmacist education in the early twentieth century and treatment of alcoholism in the mid-twentieth century.

Inevitably, questions about her life story remained unanswered. For example, how was it that my patrician grandmother (at least in her eyes) had come to marry a man out of her class, and five and a half years younger than she, when he was 17 and she was 22? Despite a diligent search, I could find nothing about their wedding except its location, which was not where I expected it to be. Consequently, I used my imagination, shaped by what I did know, to close gaps in their story. That makes Part I a work of creative nonfiction which blends my grandmother's stories, my research, and my imagination.

Part II relays my grandmother's story subsequent to my birth in 1945. The voice shifts from the third person in Part I to the first person in Part II. In essence, Part II is a memoir about my grandmother and me. The characters introduced in Part I who were alive in 1945 (my grandfather, my grandmother's sisters, known collectively to my sisters and me as the Aunts, my parents, my sisters, and our beloved maid, Ada) are all part of the continuing story that concludes with my grandmother's death in 1987. Although I have invented dialogue and certain scenes as devices to move the story forward, unlike the imagined events in Part I, the events in Part II are grounded in my memories.

Overall, I hope this work conveys how my grandparents'

lives were shaped by the region where they were born, by the historical and cultural times in which they lived, and—most of all—how their love for me, and mine for them, enriched all of our lives.

LIST OF CHARACTERS

There are **four Helens** in this story, spanning four generations:

1. Me, Helen Brooks Regan, 1945-
2. My mother, Helen Lewis Brooks, 1917-1995
3. My great aunt, my grandmother's sister, Helen Townsend Wisehart Stabler, 1882-1976
4. My great-grandmother, my grandmother's mother, Helen Jones Townsend, 1858-1951

Other major characters:

1. My grandmother, Jessie Townsend Lewis, known to us grandchildren as WooWoo, later shortened to Woo
2. My grandfather, Milton Parks Lewis, known to his wife and daughter as Empy (M.P.), and to us grandchildren as Papoo
3. My grandmother's parents, James Porter Townsend and Helen Jones Townsend, the first Helen (see above)
4. My grandmother Jessie's siblings, listed in descending birth order: Charles, Katherine (Kate), Helen, the second

Helen (see above) known as Aunt Helen to us grandchildren, Mary (Nanny), Eva (Beba), Jim. My grandmother was the sixth of seven children. An eighth child, Robley, died in infancy.

5. Mozelle, the African-American servant in my grandmother's childhood home, and Floyd, her son
6. Ada, the African-American maid in my grandmother's adult household as my mother grew up, and later in my mother's adult household as I grew up
7. My parents, Helen Townsend Lewis Brooks, (the third Helen; see above), and Richard Ensign Brooks
8. My sisters in descending birth order: Marion, Jessie, and Amy

A family tree is included in the appendix.

Part 1

Jessie

(1892-1952)

Jessie and Floyd's Canoe

Courtesy of Worcester County Library Special Collections, Snow Hill, Maryland

1.1

Frog Legs and Embezzlement

Jessie snuck down the back stairs into the kitchen.

"Mozelle," she said softly, "I'm going to get us some frog legs for supper. Be ready!"

"Chile, you's gettin' too old to go out dere in dat canoe. I'm sorry Charlie ever showed you how to paddle and shoot. And now your brother's a married man and not here to take you in hand! Now you ain't goin' with Floyd, is you? Dat's a peck o' trouble waitin' to happen, dat is!"

"You worry too much," Jessie scoffed and ducked out the screen door, making sure not to let it bang. It would be better if Mother didn't see her setting off.

The summer sun was rising and burning the mist off the Pocomoke River. Soon the bullfrogs would be sunning themselves on downed logs and croaking loudly. A perfect day for hunting. She stopped in the shed behind the house to grab the shotgun and ammunition, then headed for the river a few blocks away.

The canoe was waiting for her on the bank—and Floyd too, she hoped. It was his day off. The Collins family treated their Colored folk pretty well; not every servant got days off beyond Sunday, but Floyd got an extra day every month. He had come to her house with his mother Mozelle as an infant tied to her back; she and Floyd had learned to walk at the same time, talk at the same time, and lost teeth at the same time. Then three years ago, when they were ten, he was sent off to work for the Collinses. But she and Floyd were friends for life no matter what anyone said, and they cherished rare opportunities to continue their adventures.

Floyd was pacing back and forth impatiently when she reached the bank. He grinned broadly when he saw her. Prince, the Collinses Chesapeake Bay retriever who always accompanied them on these frog hunting trips, wagged his tail excitedly. Floyd had already placed the paddles in the canoe along with a bucket to hold their catch. Now he untied it from the dock. Jessie and Prince climbed in while he held it steady; then he joined her, barely rocking the canoe as he settled in the bow. With a shove, they were off.

It was tricky business, this shooting of bullfrogs. For one thing, the minute you fired the shotgun, they all dove into the water so one shot was all you'd get for a while. For another, the recoil from the gun would rock the canoe and propel it backward, dumping you out if you weren't careful. And for a third, once you had steadied yourself, you had to prepare for potential upset when you signaled to Prince that he could jump in the water to retrieve the frogs. But Jessie, Floyd, and Prince were all experts.

Jessie's father was Cashier, the second ranking officer, at The First National Bank. To his mortification, the Bank had recently been audited and a serious cash shortage had been revealed. While most in town dismissed out of hand the possibility that James Townsend was complicit in the embezzlement in any way, no satisfactory explanation had emerged—

nor were there any suspects. Local gossips were beginning to whisper that, even if Mr. Townsend was not directly responsible, as Cashier, he should have caught on long before the audit. The strain of this situation had created much stress at home.

Reluctant to head home despite their full bucket, Jessie and Floyd were drifting contentedly while Jessie bemoaned the unfortunate family situation. As she was protesting the injustice of suspicion being cast upon her father, they drifted past the old Nassawango Iron Furnace, which had been an important site for iron smelting through the Revolutionary War. Long ago abandoned and always silent and spooky, it was the legendary hideout of Patty Cannon and her pirate crew. Floyd and Jessie shuddered deliciously as it came into view. Then, to their surprise, they heard voices amplified over the water.

"I told you that audit would ...," said one voice.

"What do we do now?" said a second.

"We should dig up the money and ...," said a third.

Jessie and Floyd looked at each other in astonishment. Jessie nodded her head toward a small inlet that would take them closer to the Furnace. Floyd shook his head vigorously, but she paddled silently into the inlet. She brought the canoe up to a large log and began to climb out, handing the paddle and rope to Floyd. "Tie up here," she said. "I have to see if we can identify them."

Concealed by cattails, Jessie slipped into the shallow water and crept beside the log until she could see the whispering men. To her horror, she recognized one of them as her father's trusted secretary, Mr. Collins, and another as his brother, Paul Collins, the man who employed Floyd. Keeping the log between her and the bank, Jessie snuck back to the canoe. She signaled to Floyd to paddle quietly away while she clung to the side. Once they were far enough away to risk making noise, she hauled herself aboard, sputtering to Floyd, "You will never believe what I saw!"

Floyd's eyes widened when Jessie told him whom she had seen and what she had heard.

"Miss Jessie, don't tell me no more!" he exclaimed, holding his hand up as a signal to stop. "If Mr. Collins ever knows dat I knowed, no tellin' what would happen to me and Mama and Pappy."

Jessie stopped talking abruptly. Floyd was right—no matter how enlightened the Collins family was, there was no doubt they would not hesitate to sacrifice a Colored family to protect themselves. Exactly what form that sacrifice would take, neither she nor Floyd could bear thinking about. She changed the subject abruptly.

"Does Mozelle know you went hunting with me today?"

"No," Floyd responded. "I didn' leave 'til she had gone to your house." He didn't need to remind her that Mozelle had forbidden Floyd to be in Jessie's company, especially alone. And all of a sudden, they both knew she was right. They had to conceal Floyd's participation in this outing.

"All right, good," Jessie said. "I'll tell Mozelle the canoe tipped when I was fishing out frogs to explain why I am soaking wet. I think we better dump most of them before we dock because if I bring too many home, she'll think I had help."

Regretfully, but without hesitation, she threw half their catch into the river while Floyd restrained a very confused Prince to prevent him from retrieving the frogs a second time.

Fifty yards from the dock, Jessie signaled to Floyd to pull into another little inlet.

"You get out here," she said. "We don't want anyone seeing us pull into the dock together."

Nimbly, Floyd stepped out of the canoe onto the bank.

"Bye, Miss Jessie," he said softly.

"Bye, Floyd," she responded with a catch in her throat.

They would never be in a canoe together again—and they both knew it.

Jessie docked the canoe and faced the dilemma of getting out without Floyd to steady it for her. Holding tight to the bow rope and using the paddle to straddle the gunnels as a grip, she slowly pushed herself into a crouching position and then swung her hips quickly toward the dock. She landed with a plop, keeping her tight hold on the rope as the canoe scooted away from her. Climbing to her feet, she walked the canoe to the piling where it was always tied up.

"My goodness, chile!" Mozelle exclaimed when she walked through the back door into the kitchen. "What happened to you?!"

"I fell in trying to retrieve the frogs," she replied as she handed the bucket to Mozelle. "I didn't get too many."

"I told you not to go huntin' by yourself. You're lucky de current didn't take de canoe!"

"I know, but I am a good swimmer," she said defensively, feeling extraordinarily relieved to receive a scolding for going alone.

"Well, no more!" Mozelle said. She gave Jessie the same evil eye she had used since Jessie and Floyd were toddlers. The message had been unmistakable then and was now—*Do what I say right this minute!* "Now scoot upstairs and change those clothes before your mother sees you."

As Jessie scooted toward the stairs, Mozelle added, "I'll tell your mother Samson brought dese frogs by, and we'll have a nice supper."

"Oh, Mozelle," she said, gratefully accepting the hug Mozelle offered as a gesture of peace despite her wet clothes.

At lunch, Jessie's brother Jim was full of talk about baseball and horse racing, his two favorite topics. Usually annoyed by Jim's domination of mealtime conversation, today she was grateful for his cover. Mother was asking him for details about the Colored team that was coming to town. She loved baseball too—in fact, the whole family did. Mother was eager to learn if Judy Johnson, the famous third baseman, was on this team.

While they talked, her mind was racing. She had decided to tell Father the truth about what she had seen and heard, minus the part about Floyd's presence of course. She didn't know if he would believe such a fantastic tale, but they had a special relationship. She was the last of the five girls, and Father had always had a soft spot for her—to the annoyance of her sisters. Their relationship had become even closer as the older girls had left the house.

But how to get Father alone? After lunch, he would walk back to the bank; she was supposed to go to her room to read quietly during the heat of the summer afternoon. The only solution she could see was to catch up with him before he reached the bank, but to do that, she needed to sneak out without Mother or Jim seeing her. Mozelle would help.

The timing was delicate. If she snuck down the back stairs

too soon before Mother and Jim were settled, she would have impossible explaining to do. If she waited too long, Father would reach the bank before she caught up to him. It was only three blocks away. She counted to 100 and then snuck down the back stairs for the second time that day. Mozelle was startled to see her, but she hushed when she saw Jessie's finger at her lips.

"I have to catch Father. I have something very important to tell him."

"Chile, what ....?"

"Please Mozelle, just pretend you don't see me. Just turn around and wash the dishes." And she slipped out the screen door, once more making sure it closed silently.

It was very hot now, and humid, but she had to run once she snuck through the herb garden, around the side of the house to the street. She was thankful that curtains were drawn over neighbors' street side windows to shield the interiors from the scorching sun.

It was indeed hot, so Father was walking slowly. When she was about half of a block behind him, she called out as loudly as she dared, "Father." And again, "Father." He turned around, even more surprised to see her than Mozelle had been.

"What?"

"I have something very important—and private—to tell you. I couldn't think of any other way to get you alone ..."

"You are scarlet with heat. We must find shade," he said as he led her to a bench under a graceful mimosa tree.

"I know Mother told me not to go out in the canoe," she began. "Please don't tell her...,"

He looked at her sternly, but simultaneously handed her

his handkerchief to wipe her dripping face. There was nothing to do now but plunge ahead, so she told him her tale.

At dinner, as Mozelle was serving frog legs and Mother was exclaiming about how wonderful it was for Samson to share his bounty, the telephone rang. Everyone jumped. The telephone didn't ring very often because there weren't many other families or businesses that had one. Theirs had been installed about a month before at the direction of Governor Smith, still President of First National Bank, which he had founded about twenty years earlier. Father, as Cashier, ran the bank while Governor Smith pursued his political career. He had been very understanding about the missing money, but the embezzlement still reflected very badly on the family.

"I will answer it," Father said. "Excuse me."

No one took another bite as the drone of Father's voice drifted in from the front hall. Even Mozelle stood stock still, a platter of frog legs in hand.

As Father took his seat, he said, "That was Governor Smith telephoning to tell me that the missing money has been returned. A citizen was canoeing by the old Nassawango Furnace and overheard the embezzlers talking as they buried the money there. The sheriff went to the Furnace and found the money exactly where the citizen said it would be. He will remain anonymous just in case the thieves get any ideas about retribution. Even I do not know who this fine person is."

Jessie sat in shock, willing her face to remain impassive. Father had believed her, retrieved the money, and was now protecting her.

And to Mozelle, he said, "See that Jessie gets as many frog legs as she might like. I know she loves them."

As she bent over to serve Jessie, Mozelle whispered, "Chile, I declare."

Out loud she said, "Here, chile, take as many o' dese as you want."

"Thank you," Jessie replied. She and Mozelle locked eyes to seal a secret that would last a lifetime.

Old Furnace Town where Jessie and Floyd overheard the embezzlers

Courtesy of Worcester County Library Special Collections, Snow Hill, Maryland

1.2

Football, Pirates, and Soldiers

Jessie could not fall asleep. She had eaten her share of oyster stew, roast goose, spoon bread, and pumpkin pie, but indigestion wasn't the problem. Tomorrow, November 27, 1902, was the twelfth meeting of the Army-Navy football game at Franklin Field in Philadelphia. Her sisters, Helen and Mary, were traveling by train with Governor and Mrs. Smith, Senator Moore, the Richardsons, Father, and many other friends from Snow Hill to attend the game. They had to leave very early, and she intended to be up to see them off. The travelers had their own car on the train and, if she was lucky, she would be able to board the car and sit in the velvet seats even if only briefly. Mother had said that at ten years old, Jessie was too young to attend, but she was bubbling over with excitement just the same.

The New York, Philadelphia, and Norfolk Railroad Station was decorated with red, white, and blue bunting, and a huge banner proclaiming Go Navy! hung from the ceiling of the waiting room. The railroad, opened twenty years before in 1884, extended from New York, through Philadelphia, Wilmington, and Baltimore, and then through Snow Hill, across the Virginia state line, and through the new town of Parksley, all the way to the tip of the Delmarva Peninsula to another new town, Cape Charles. The new harbor there was created from the dredging of the channel between Kings and Plantation Creeks. Once in Cape Charles, both passengers and freight could board the ferry for an easy trip to Norfolk or Hampton. Economic, social, and political activity had exploded on the Eastern Shore with the completion of the railroad and the harbor. Famous Chincoteague oysters and other seafood, lumber, iron products—all manner of things could now be shipped easily to large northeastern markets. The election of Snow Hill native John Smith as Governor of Maryland in 1899 and, later, US Senator exemplified the astounding increase in the prosperity and influence of the region stimulated by the arrival of the railroad. The celebratory send-off of the Governor's Army-Navy party from the Snow Hill Train Station was an event of immense civic pride.

The Naval Academy in Annapolis had long been easily accessible from Snow Hill traveling by steamer down the Pocomoke River into the Chesapeake Bay and then across to the western shore of the Bay and up to Annapolis. With the advent of the train, Philadelphia was now accessible too. The Richardsons' son Thomas was one of many Snow Hill sons to matriculate at the Academy, but this year he became the first to play a solo trumpet in the Navy Marching Band—and the first to travel by train to perform at the Army-Navy game.

Sister Kate, who was also staying home, maneuvered Jessie deftly through a crowd gathered to send off the contingent of local fans. They reached the Governor's car and scrambled on board. Father, who had boarded earlier with the Governor and the Richardsons, took Jessie's hand eagerly.

"Governor," he said, "may I introduce my youngest daughter, Jessie? And you remember my oldest, Katherine. She accompanied us two years ago for the tenth anniversary game."

"Oh, yes indeed. How do you do, Katherine? I'm sorry we couldn't accommodate you again this year," the Governor replied.

"And you, young lady. Your turn will come soon enough," he said as he smiled and bent down to take Jessie's hand.

"Thank you, sir. But I wish I was going today to hear Thomas Richardson play the trumpet!"

The Governor chuckled. "Well, perhaps by the time you attend, a Snow Hill boy will be the quarterback of the team!"

"Go along now, Jessie," Father urged. "The train will leave soon, and I know you'd be delighted to be aboard when it does!"

Jessie and Kate climbed off the train and headed home. "Please wake me up with the news if I fall asleep before everyone gets home," she pleaded as she and Kate strolled along.

Kate draped her arm on Jessie's shoulders and gave her a quick squeeze. "I promise," she said.

Navy lost the game that year, but her sisters' descriptions of the roar of the crowd, the midshipmen in dress uniforms, the band marching, and Thomas Richardson's soaring solo at halftime pushed the score into insignificance. The pageant was what was important, and Jessie's memories would be as vivid as if she had actually stowed away on the Governor's car and attended the game herself.

Early in the new year of 1903, the household stirred with excitement in anticipation of the arrival of George Alfred Townsend, Jessie's cousin. Mr. Townsend had been a news-

Helen #4 at the War Correspondents Memorial at Gathland, now a Maryland State Park

paper correspondent during the Civil War. Now he was a writer whose commentary on current affairs appeared in major newspapers in Baltimore, Philadelphia, and even New York. Under the pen name GATH, he also wrote fiction. The mayor of Pocomoke City had invited Mr. Townsend back to his hometown to give a public reading of his soon-to-be published novel *Talbot's Hawks*, and Mr. Townsend asked to visit his cousins while he was on the Eastern Shore. In anticipation of his visit, Mother had been reading his famous novel *The Entailed Hat* aloud in the evenings after dinner. Jessie was particularly taken by the character Samson, the Colored man who ran so fast that he could catch rabbits on foot. She wondered if Floyd could do the same thing. She made a mental note to challenge him when she saw him next.

Cousin George entranced the entire family with stories as they sat in front of the parlor stove after dinner. Jim had asked for war stories, but Cousin George demurred. Antietam was too bloody to talk about, he said, and because he could never get his mind past it, he just wouldn't talk about the war.

In any case, stories about the Civil War could not have been more exciting than the stories he did tell. First he told about Mr. Hawke who had killed the King's revenue collector in Maryland for taxing colonists unfairly. This was years before the Revolutionary War, and foreshadowed Maryland's readiness to join the rebellion when it arose. Jessie was thrilled to think that someone from Maryland had stood up against taxation without representation long before the Boston Tea Party.

Cousin George went on to tell stories about Patty Cannon, who had harbored pirates in a road house on the Delaware/Maryland border. He told about Bluebeard, who had taken refuge from the British in various river deltas including the Pocomoke in the Chesapeake Bay. Mother told stories about Patty Cannon's ghost appearing at the local Nassawango Iron Furnace. Patty and Bluebeard were alleged to have taken refuge there more than once. Even though Jessie and Jim had heard these stories before, they could not take their eyes off Cousin George as he told tales of those pirates hunkered down just a few miles from their house. Jessie shivered, unobserved by the others she hoped, while she recalled her recent caper at the Furnace with Floyd. She and Jim were reluctant to say goodbye to Cousin George when he boarded the train back to Philadelphia the next day.

In September, Mother astounded Jessie with the proposition that she might be able to miss school for a couple days to visit Cousin George at his estate, Gathland. Located on South Mountain in Western Maryland, he sought refuge there from the sweltering heat and humidity of Washington, DC during the summer.

"You know that it takes almost half a day to reach Baltimore on our shopping trips," she warned. "To get to Gathland, once we travel by steamer down the Pocomoke River and up the Chesapeake to Baltimore, we will have to transfer to the Western Maryland Railroad for another two hours, and then take a carriage for the last few miles. It will be a very long trip."

"But this visit is special," she continued. "Cousin George has invited us for an important occasion. We've been invited to see the march of the Fourth United States Field Artillery Battery E, through Gathland as it goes on its way to dedicate a memorial to the New Jersey battalion at Antietam."

The battery commander knew that Cousin George had been at Antietam when the battery had fought there in 1862, she explained, and that he had built a monument to all Civil War correspondents at Gathland. The commander had planned the march so participants could pay tribute to the brave journalists who had reported on the battle.

"Would you mind missing school?" Mother wondered aloud.

Jessie loved school, but she had no doubt that sacrificing her perfect attendance record for this occasion was a trivial matter.

"Yes, yes. I mean no, I don't mind missing school, and yes, I want to go! I am not worried about the journey!" she answered excitedly.

The journey was long and exhausting. However, as she

Plaque describing how
George Alfred Townsend acquired Gathland

watched former soldiers and those marching in honor of soldiers who could not endure the trek pour into Gathland and gather at the foot of the memorial, she felt sure that even the Army-Navy game had not been as grand as this. She was proud that Cousin George had thought to have gallons of cider available to quench the marchers' thirst on this warm September day.

Later that evening, Jessie was mesmerized as the family gathered in Uncle George's living room to hear his stories again. This time he did speak about the journalists, insisting that they could be considered braver than the soldiers because they carried only pen and paper for defense. He asked them if they had heard about *The Red Badge of Courage* by

Stephen Crane, which vividly depicts the horror of a Civil War battle. Cousin George said the book's success led many newspapers to hire Mr. Crane as a correspondent to report on foreign wars all over the world. So you could say that the Gathland memorial honored him too. Cousin George deeply regretted that Mr. Crane had died of tuberculosis just a few years before at age twenty-eight. "Too young," Cousin George said, "much too young."

Two months later, on her eleventh birthday, Jessie's eyes lit up with excitement as she opened a copy of *The Red Badge of Courage.*

"Check the flyleaf," Mother said.

There she read *To Jessie, so that she will always remember her day at Gathland. Love, Cousin George.*

1.3

KATE

Four years separated Eva, the last of the older six children, and Jessie, and then another four years separated her from Jim. Jessie often felt like she and Jim were afterthoughts. Mother had taught all four older girls to do cross-stitch, and they had each made special samplers that now hung on the living room walls. But no matter how hard Jessie begged, her mother had yet to teach her. She hadn't even given her a middle name, which made her feel indignant every time she thought about it. Father called her his "special girl" and told her it was his lucky day when she was born. Mother never said anything like that. From Mother's perspective, Jessie and Jim were the last shake of the bag.

Jessie's older siblings did compensate for their mother's neglect to some extent. Charlie, the oldest, often took her and Jim out in his canoe. He showed them how to handle a shotgun, how to hunt for bullfrogs and ducks, and how to work the Chesapeake Bay retrievers who were strong swimmers that loved fetching the prey. By the time Charlie got married and left home, Jessie and Jim could confidently head out on the Pocomoke River on their own.

Kate was Jessie's favorite sister. She thought that Kate was the most beautiful of them all. Jessie liked to lounge on her sister's bed while Kate brushed her long auburn hair. Frequently Kate would seat Jessie at the dressing table and brush her hair too. Jessie loved Kate's gentle touch, pretending for a few moments that Kate was her mother, not her big sister. On the day her eighth grade class was to be photographed, Kate made sure Mozelle had ironed Jessie's favorite dress with the sailor collar, and helped her slip it on without causing a wrinkle. Then Kate had brushed her hair specially, braided it, and tied the tip with a silk bow. Jessie had been proud to sit in the front row for the photograph, being very, very careful not to move a muscle. She was tempted to giggle while the photographer worked under his black hood, but, thankfully, she suppressed that urge. The resulting photograph showed a girl of about twelve sitting ramrod straight, gazing forward from large, round eyes, with hair pulled back to display a high forehead, and with feet primly crossed at the ankles.

On one frosty morning, Kate suggested that she, Jessie, and Jim go ice skating. Jessie and Jim had both been on skates the year before. Jessie had learned quickly, but Jim had fallen often. He would brush off the hand Kate offered to steady him, embarrassed that his big sister was gliding around so gracefully. Jessie wondered if she would again glide gracefully, and if now, a year later, Jim would develop more skill and confidence. Kate encouraged them, saying that skating was like canoeing—once you learned, you didn't forget. *That bodes well for me,* Jessie thought—but she wasn't sure about Jim.

As it turned out, Jim did take to skating much more easily this year. The two of them set up an obstacle course and raced pell-mell from one end to the other.

"Kate," Jessie called. "Come on. I bet I can beat both of you."

Kate had been hanging on the sidelines, unusual for her, although Jessie hadn't really noticed.

"Okay," she replied. "I'll try."

"One, two, three—go!" Jim cried, and off they went. Within a few yards, Kate began coughing and glided to a stop with her head down.

"I'm sorry," she said once the coughing eased. "I'm feeling tired and cold. I think we should go home."

Jessie stole a glance at Jim who said immediately, "Okay, Kate," as he skated up to her and took her hand. When they got home, Jessie went up with Kate to her room, helped her into a nightdress, and sat down next to her on the edge of the bed. Jim sent Mozelle up with a steaming cup of chamomile tea.

"Here, chile," Mozelle said. "Dis here tea soothes any cough."

"Thank you, Mozelle," Kate said as she took a tiny sip. "Now you all go on while I have a little rest." She let her head fall back on the pillows, and Jessie tried not to notice that her face was as white as the sheets.

Back down in the kitchen, Mozelle reassured them. "Just a winter chill. She'll be right as rain."

Kate was not right as rain. Over the next few weeks her coughing spells became longer and more frequent, and she spent increasing amounts of time in bed. Uncle Paul, Mother's brother and the local doctor in Snow Hill, had tried several different remedies, none of which had helped. One afternoon as Jessie sat next to Kate's bed reading to her, Mother entered with Uncle Paul.

"Jessie, please step outside while Uncle Paul examines Kate," she instructed. With a lump in her throat, Jessie took a seat on the stairs outside Kate's room.

Mother was talking to Uncle Paul as they opened the door to leave. Jessie couldn't make out their words, but she couldn't mistake the somber tone of their voices. With an even larger lump in her throat, she climbed back up the stairs to resume reading to Kate. Coughing badly, Kate tried to hide the handkerchief she removed from her mouth as Jessie entered, but she was not quick enough. Jessie was horrified to see what she was sure was a spot of blood.

Just then her mother appeared at the door. "Jessie," she said sternly, "you come away now."

"But ..."

"Do not disobey me. Come away now."

In the hallway, Mother took her hand with an uncharacteristically gentle touch. "Uncle Paul says Kate is very, very sick and, for everyone's good health, only Helen and I, who will take turns nursing her, can be in the room with her. I'm even going to tell Mozelle to stay away."

Her mother re-entered Kate's room, and Jessie stumbled down the back stairs to the warm sanctuary of Mozelle's arms.

"What is it, chile?" Mozelle asked softly as she dried Jessie's tears with her apron.

"Oh, Mozelle. Uncle Paul says Kate is very, very sick. We can't go into her room anymore—even you can't."

Mozelle folded Jessie against her and swayed gently. "Chile, chile, dis is so hard. We must ask de good Lord to look after dis family."

Jessie, third from right in front row, graduating from 8th grade, wearing dress and ribbon prepared by Kate.

Courtesy of Worcester County Library Special Collections, Snow Hill, Maryland

Several days later, at the dinner table, Mother asked for everyone's attention. Jessie's heart dropped. "Tomorrow," she said, "Uncle Paul and Helen will accompany Kate to the hospital at Johns Hopkins University in Baltimore. It's one of the finest hospitals in the world, and Kate will receive the very best care. Uncle Paul will come home, but, as a trained nurse, your sister will stay with her."

"Will she get better, Mother?" Jessie asked anxiously.

"She will be getting the very best care," Mother repeated, but this was not the reply Jessie yearned to hear.

Several weeks later, without any news of Kate's improvement, Mother made another announcement at dinner. This time she named Kate's disease, and answered the question Jessie had not dared to voice.

"Kate is very sick with tuberculosis," Mother said. "She is being moved to a sanitarium in Lake Saranac, New York, where the clear air is very beneficial to patients with this awful disease. Helen will go with her."

Father broke the hush around the table. "Let us bow our heads in prayer and ask the Lord to heal our daughter and sister, Kate—and to preserve our daughter and sister Helen in her time of service."

With sudden shock, Jessie realized that Father was worried Helen could be taken ill too. As she bowed her head, she noticed that even Jim had tears welling in his eyes.

Months went by. Spring became summer. Neither of her other two sisters offered to brush her hair, but she didn't particularly want them to. School was out. Jim was off playing baseball with his pals, hanging around the stables at the race track, doing whatever boys do. She didn't blame him. Their lives had been diverging even before Kate became sick, but the house felt so empty when he bolted out the door after breakfast. Jim, her companion throughout her childhood, had new friends now, and Kate, the mother in her heart, was far away fighting a terrifying illness.

Mozelle scooped her up for a huge comforting hug at least once a day. She did not try to console Jessie with words, but her touch was always soothing. However, when Jessie left the kitchen, the huge pit in her stomach reopened. She tried to read and write letters to Kate, but her concentration flagged. At least weekly during lunch, Mother read the latest letter from Helen, which conveyed things like *Kate enjoys the food,* and *the view of the Adirondack Mountains from the veranda is breathtaking,* but never that Kate was much improved. Jessie could lose herself for an hour or so playing the piano, but nothing dispelled the feeling of dread in her heart.

In August, 1905, Mother announced at dinner that she was going to Lake Saranac to relieve Helen, who was coming home for a desperately needed rest. Helen, as the oldest, would be in charge of the household, and Mother expected them all to cooperate with her. She would be gone for an unknown period of time. No one asked how she would know when it was time to return because they knew she would return with Kate one way or another. Father asked them to bow their heads for the special prayer of intercession he had been offering every day since Kate was taken to Lake Saranac. This time he asked the Lord to watch over them and to protect Mother.

To Jessie's surprise, one evening after Helen returned, she offered to brush Jessie's hair. "Kate asked me to look after you," Helen said. "She told me that the two of you enjoyed special time when she brushed your hair." Tears welled up in Jessie's eyes, and, quite spontaneously, Helen sprang forward to embrace her. Other than Mozelle, no one had touched her since that day so many months before when Mother had gently taken her hand to explain the seriousness of Kate's illness. At first Jessie flinched, but then she relaxed. Here was a gift from Kate, and she would accept it.

As it turned out, Mother was gone for two months. Kate's funeral was held immediately upon her return. Jessie attended, but heard not a word, did not sing a hymn, did not register a single face at the luncheon following the service. She felt she had died too.

Several days after attending her big sister's funeral, Jessie came upon Kate's obituary as she despondently leafed through the local paper. *Struck down too young—only 24,* it said, *despite the heroic efforts of a tuberculosis expert called in from Philadelphia two weeks before the end came.* Jessie had no tears left. Instead she was angry—angry at herself, at Jim, at Kate for going ice skating nine months ago. That's when the cough really started. *If only we hadn't gone, maybe Kate would still be alive.*

On a chilly, grey November day, the family gathered at Kate's grave for the dedication of her headstone, *Katherine Porter Townsend, 1881-1905.* The stone was spectacular—engraved lavishly with angels, lilies, draperies, and all manner of flourishes. So pointless, Jessie thought. Nothing could ever be as beautiful as Kate herself. Evidently others agreed. No headstone in the family plot ever matched the elegance of Kate's.

1.4

Father

Father had promised his daughters continuing education after high school if they wanted it. Helen and Eva had chosen nursing school, and Mary had chosen secretarial school, but Jessie preferred a liberal arts college. Father had demurred, so Jessie chose Goldey-Beacom Business School in Wilmington, Delaware, as her second choice. She hoped she could persuade him to reconsider a liberal arts college after a successful year at Goldey-Beacom. Nonetheless, to her surprise as she walked into her first stenography class, she found herself somewhat excited at the prospect of learning the meaning of all those swirly symbols. She knew Father, who loved her dearly, believed this was the right path. *Maybe he was right,* she thought.

One day several weeks into the term, Jessie was startled when Mrs. Goldey appeared at the door of the classroom and said, "Excuse me, Mrs. Jackson, but I need Jessie Townsend to come with me."

As they walked to the office, Mrs. Goldey said, "Your sister Eva is on the phone."

Jessie didn't need to be told that this was an extraordinary event. First of all, phone calls for students were rare, and second of all, Mrs. Goldey never interrupted a class. Although she felt a tinge of alarm as she picked up the receiver, mostly she was annoyed at being pulled from stenography class. It was crucial not to miss the new characters as they were being introduced.

"Jessie," Eva said with a tremor in her voice.

"Whatever is the matter?" Jessie responded a bit briskly, unable to repress her annoyance.

"Father is dead," Eva said. Silence. Finally Eva spoke again. "You must come home. Father's funeral is in two days."

Jessie simply hung up and stood rooted to the floor. What Eva had said was not possible. Kate's death was the exception. Tragedy could not strike a second time, especially not to Father, who was in the prime of life and who was the core of the family. What would happen to them?

"Jessie," Mrs. Goldey had come around the counter that separated the office staff from the public and had laid a hand gently on her arm. "What is it?"

Jessie slowly looked up. "Father is dead. I must go home."

She did not feel Mrs. Goldey's hug, nor did she remember the ride in Mr. Goldey's motorcar to the train station. Only when she saw Mozelle waiting for her when she disembarked in Snow Hill did the numbness lift.

"Chile, chile, dis is de worse," Mozelle said as Jessie sobbed in her arms.

When Jessie had arrived home, Mother did not reach out to her, did not speak, did not even nod her head to acknowledge Jessie's arrival. At the time of Kate's diagnosis, Mother had at least taken her hand. On the train ride home, Jessie had dared to hope for some gesture of affection and sympathy from her mother in the face of this catastrophe, but

Jessie's father
James Porter Townsend

clearly that hope had been in vain. She followed Mozelle to the sanctuary of the kitchen.

Evidently Father had awakened with a headache, but he and Eva, who now worked as a teller, walked together to the bank two blocks up the street as they did every morning. No sooner had they arrived than Father had turned around and walked home with Eva watching him anxiously every step of the way. As soon as he entered the house, he collapsed with a violent headache. Mother sent Mozelle running for Uncle Paul while Jim helped her get Father into bed. Uncle Paul gave him his headache powder, but told Mother he was not sure it would help. He was right. A few hours later, Father had an attack of apoplexy that rendered him unconscious and he died by evening. Uncle Paul kept apologizing to Mother, saying he was so sorry that he didn't have any way to treat severe apoplexy.

Jessie sat in the family pew with her six siblings and her mother. Father's brothers and all of Mother's family sat just behind them. Reverend Prettyman eagerly recited Father's entire life history. He described how he was a member of the third generation of Townsends to be buried there in the Whatcoat Methodist Cemetery along with two of the fourth generation—Kate and their infant brother Robley. The Reverend described how Father had married Mother in 1878; how her family, the Joneses, also had several generations buried there; how she and Father had eight children together. He talked about Father's early days running Grandfather's farm on the Acquando Branch of the Pocomoke. Though Reverend Prettyman would never mention such things, Jessie couldn't help but think of Floyd, whose grandparents had worked on the farm as Grandfather's slaves.

In his sonorous voice, Reverend Prettyman continued, "We all remember Brother Townsend as general manager of the Smith, Moore, Richardson store. We remember that Governor Smith appointed him Cashier of The First National Bank here in Snow Hill when the Governor obtained its charter in 1887. We are grateful for his stewardship of our church, and we know that our town is poorer for his untimely death at fifty-six." For the briefest moment, Jessie felt a surge of pride sweep over her feelings of grief.

The pallbearers steered Father's coffin down the aisle and placed it in the hearse for the short journey to the cemetery. Everyone followed on foot. It was such an honor to have former Governor, now Senator, John Smith as an honorary pallbearer. The First National Bank, across the street, was draped in black. During calling hours at home before the service, Senator Smith had told Mother that the Bank could never replace Father, who was such an honest and reliable Cashier. Mother had proudly told them that Senator Smith

First National Bank where James was Cashier

Courtesy of Worcester County Library Special Collections, Snow Hill, Maryland

had respected Father from the first day he had been hired at the new bank almost seventeen years ago.

As they stood at the edge of the grave and as Reverend Prettyman eulogized Father one more time, Jessie's eyes wandered. There was Kate's tombstone just a few feet away; her mind drifted to that other autumn day five years previously in 1905 when they had buried her beloved sister. Perhaps memories of Kate could dull the newly returned ache in her heart. She blocked out Reverend Prettyman's voice as best she could. By imagining Kate was brushing her hair once again, she returned temporarily to an earlier time of safety and security.

Slowly she realized Eva was whispering in her ear. "It's time to go. Everyone is walking to the house."

Jessie walked home too. She took her place in the receiving line in the parlor. She must have eaten something from the bountiful buffet that Mozelle was overseeing in the dining room. She must have walked up to her room and gotten in bed. But the next morning, all she could remember was sitting at Father's graveside and dreaming about Kate brushing her hair. All she could feel was dread. *What would happen now?*

1.5

Empy

Father's death induced a second dark, heavy cloud that obscured the future. Did she even have a future? How long would it take before this new dark cloud would dissipate? Four years, as it had for the cloud induced by Kate's death?

Shortly before Father died, Jessie had emerged from under the cloud of Kate's death. She had enjoyed her senior year in high school in 1909, when she had immersed herself in the Declamation Contest. In the first round, she had recited *I Hear America Singing* by Walt Whitman, a performance which catapulted her into the final round. To prepare, not only did she rehearse, but she bobbed her hair, regretting for just a moment the loss of the braid Kate had once so lovingly woven as they sat at her dressing table. She talked Mother into taking her to Baltimore to shop for a dress in the new dropped-waist style.

Jessie's new, modern look boosted her confidence. She was proud to recite the story of legendary Marylander Tench Tilghman, General Washington's aide-de-camp. She was exhilarated to describe his thrilling ride to Philadelphia to inform the Continental Congress of Cornwallis's surrender at Yorktown. Her performance reciting the essay *Tench Tilghman's Ride* in the final round of the Declamation Contest was a triumph.

At the end of that summer, she and her sister Eva had spent two weeks at the Sea Crest Inn in Ocean City where they raced pell-mell across the hot sand to dive under the waves. And was it really only a few months since she and Edwin Richardson had sung their duet at the Purnell Hotel before an enthusiastic audience? And only one month since she had left for Wilmington to begin the two-year course of study at Goldey Commercial College, following in Eva's footsteps?

Two years after Father's death, on a warm September afternoon in 1912, Jessie was reading an article in the Society section of *The Baltimore Sun* titled "Before School Takes In." It listed her along with Nora, Emily, Mollie, Bessie, and others as the honorees at a large party for local young people about to depart for colleges in Baltimore, Annapolis, and the fine women's colleges in Lynchburg and Sweet Briar, Virginia. These young women, her friends, were living the life she dreamed of, but which Father's death had snatched away. Now the family could not afford a college education for her—and probably not even her second year at Goldey Commercial College in Wilmington.

After Father's funeral, Senator Smith had generously agreed to underwrite the rest of her first year at Goldey. Commercial College in Wilmington. Jessie had returned there after Thanksgiving, and the following spring, she received a certificate of completion of the stenography course. Then Senator Smith had used his connections to secure a banking job for Jessie. She knew she should be grateful to Senator Smith for his generous support, but she had dreamed of asking Father to support her application to Randolph-Ma-

Young Woo

con Woman's College. There she would have plunged into the renowned theater and dance department. She would have studied Greek so that by her senior year, she would have auditioned for a role in the annual Greek play. Instead of her, it was Jessie's friend Bessie who was returning to RMWC to perform in that play. Jessie would be returning to a job she hated.

And then there was Edwin, who was returning to the Naval Academy for his second year. He continued to pay attention to her at parties, in the stands of baseball games, and on the beach at Public Landing. He had promised to write, but nothing more.

Two months later, on her twentieth birthday, Jessie was slightly happier. She had a new job which she liked better than her previous one. And she had an interesting letter from Mother who wrote that Senator Smith had bought Furnace

Town, the site of the old Nassawango Iron Furnace. Furnace Town was home to Patty Cannon's ghost and former home of Samson Hat, a character in Cousin George's popular novel, *The Entailed Hat*. It was also the site where she and Floyd had overheard the embezzlers. She would write to Bessie and suggest an outing to Furnace Town when everyone returned for vacation in the spring. Maybe if they went in the evening, they could perform a dramatic reading from *The Entailed Hat* and conjure up Samson Hat's ghost. Maybe Patty Cannon herself would pay a visit!

Two more years slipped away. Jessie gradually lost the last glimmer of hope of finding a path away from Snow Hill and out into the wider world. She had been counting on Edwin to take her hand and lead her into an exciting life, but evidently he had different plans.

Jessie anticipated Edwin's visits to Snow Hill from the Naval Academy, but when he was home, she was forced to overlook his inattentiveness compared to the very real attentiveness she had experienced during their high school years. She had felt Edwin pulling away from her through his increasingly infrequent letters; nevertheless, she had been stunned when she received the letter telling her to "to "explore the world" like he would be doing onboard his Navy ship. He was graduating and was committed to an extended period at sea. He said he couldn't predict what the future would bring. Jessie could not fool herself any longer. Her dreams of marrying Edwin were ridiculous. But if she was not going to marry Edwin, how would she ever escape the boredom and drudgery of her life?

One morning while home for one of her periodic visits,

Jessie sat in the parlor with a book lying unread in her lap. The sound of male voices in the back of the house snapped her out of her doldrums. Jim was home from the races at Public Landing. But there were two voices. Had he brought someone home with him?

"Jessie," he called, "I want you to meet my pal."

She felt the tiniest tingle of excitement. *Who was this?*

Jim walked into the parlor accompanied by a young man who was the opposite of Edwin in many ways. Where Edwin was athletic with the physique of someone who thrives on rigorous activity, this person was slender and bookish. Where Edwin filled up a room with his voice and his body, Jim's new friend seemed quiet, almost shy.

"This is Empy," Jim said. "His real name is Milton P. Lewis, but everyone calls him by his initials—M. P. He goes to Goldey Commercial College just as you did; just as I do. We met in accounting class. He's on his way home to Hallwood for spring vacation, but he's stopped to visit me for a couple of days on the way."

"Empy, this is my sister Jessie," he continued. "She's home this week from her job in Onancock."

"Hello," he said softly.

"Hello", she replied. "You must be warm after hours in the sun. I'll ask Mozelle to bring us some lemonade."

"I would enjoy that," he said.

When she returned to the parlor, Empy and Jim were sitting together looking over the racing sheet for tomorrow. Empy looked up as she entered.

She desperately wanted to start a conversation with this unexpected visitor. "I had a job in Cape Charles for about a year, and I traveled through Hallwood on my way down to Cape Charles at the tip of the Delmarva Peninsula. Oh, but you probably know that," she said, blushing slightly.

"Oh," he responded, "then you likely passed my parents' house; it sits right on the main road. And maybe you passed Nassawango High School too, a little further down the peninsula. I graduated there."

"Probably," she replied. "The Eastern Shore isn't a very big place after all. How did you find your way to Goldey College?"

"They advertised it in the local newspaper," he replied. "I don't want to be a farmer like my father, so when I saw that they train clerks for the big companies in Wilmington and Philadelphia, I knew that's where I wanted to go. I saved my money from harvesting potatoes, and now I have almost completed the commercial course."

She noted the little tinge of pride in his voice and smiled to herself. And she couldn't help remembering that Senator Smith was underwriting Jim's education at Goldey just as he had hers. Although her family lived on a much reduced income since Father's death, no one had to dig potatoes to pay for anything.

Mozelle entered with lemonade. Jim did not introduce her to Empy—that was not done. She simply went up to him with the tray, saying, "Please help youself, sir."

Empy continued. "Do you like the races as much as Jim does? Maybe you'd like to go to Public Landing with us tomorrow?"

She dared not catch Jim's eye as she responded with a half-truth. "I like baseball as much as he does (true) and racing almost as much (not at all true). I would love to go with you tomorrow."

Jim interjected: "Empy will spend the night here so we can talk more at dinner. We have other plans now, but we'll leave you the racing sheet while we're gone." He brought it over to her, raising his eyebrows as she took it. She ignored him.

After they left, Mozelle returned to fetch the empty glasses.

"Well, Miss Jessie, I declare," she said. Jessie ignored her, saying merely, "The lemonade was delicious—not too sweet."

Three days later, a short item appeared in the society section of the local paper: *Mr. Milton P. Lewis has returned to Hallwood after visiting his friend Mr. James P. Townsend, Jr.* This time, a notice in the paper brought a smile to Jessie's face. What a pleasure it had been to be in the company of a man who was gentle and soft-spoken—so unlike the brusque and loud Edwin.

Jessie, Jim, and Empy saw each other as often that summer as they could. One of their outings took them to a Hilldale Daisies baseball game. Floyd had come by recently to tell Jessie that the great Judy Johnson would be staying with them when the team came to town the next weekend. All the players and coaches would stay in the homes of local Colored folk because no hotel would accept them, and the team didn't have money for hotels. They all made just $5 a game and had to cover their expenses from that.

Floyd had nearly jumped out of his skin with excitement. Everybody, White or Colored, knew that Moses and Harriet Johnson had lived next door to Floyd's family. And everybody knew that William Julius Johnson had been born there, but that he hadn't been in town since he was eight. His family had moved to Wilmington, where his father was Director of the Athletic League for the Negro Settlement House. And everybody, both White and Colored, had followed Judy's career as he developed into the star third-baseman for the Hilldale Daisies, which now stood in first place in the Negro League.

The day of the game dawned sunny and hot. Crowds poured into the bleachers of the baseball diamond behind Snow Hill High School. Whites sat on the shady side and would have the sun to their backs for most of the game. Coloreds sat across the diamond. Luckily, the shady side was also the third base side so Jessie, Jim, and Empy would have a close view of Judy when his team was in the field. Jessie signaled to Floyd across the field, using their childhood gesture for getting each other's attention, but Floyd didn't respond. He probably couldn't see her. More likely, he decided it just wasn't safe to signal a White woman in so public a setting.

Judy did not disappoint. With the score tied and the bases loaded, Judy dove to snag a hard-hit grounder, jumped to his feet, whipped the ball to the second baseman, who whipped it to first for an inning-ending double play. Both the White crowd and the Colored crowd on opposite sides of the field leapt to their feet, roaring approval. The run from third did score, but, in the very next inning, Judy slapped a double down the right field line, scoring two runs. The Daisies won the game by one run. The White crowd was jubilant as it filed out of the bleachers, heading toward the center of town in a steady stream. The Colored crowd lingered to congratulate the players and to lead them to their homes. There, the

Helen #4 at the Negro Baseball Hall of Fame where Judy Johnson is memorialized

players could wash down with a freshly drawn bucket of cool well water and eat some down home cookin'. Jessie had no doubt that Mozelle was going all out to help organize what would be a neighborhood banquet.

Another weekend, Jessie, Jim, and Empy traveled to the Pocomoke Agricultural Fair. "Let's go in here," Jessie urged as they passed the tent bearing the sign of the US Children's Bureau. The barker was urging mothers with infants to come in for a free health examination.

"Nah," Jim said. "You go. Empy and I will meet you at the harness racing track." Off they went, and she headed into the tent.

For some time, she had been curious about the baby shows that went on at fairs like this. The local paper carried photographs of winners from fairs throughout Maryland and Delaware, and she wondered how the winners were chosen. Inside the tent a woman in a nurse's uniform greeted her.

"Would you like to enter your baby?"

Embarrassed all of a sudden, she came up with a quick lie.

"Oh no. I'm here to gather information for my sister."

"Well, here's the form we ask entrants to fill out. Let me highlight this section which asks for information about your family breeding. The Children's Bureau is now cooperating with the Eugenics Record Office directed by Dr. Charles Davenport at the Cold Spring Harbor Laboratory in Long Island, NY. The Office is collecting information to determine if the family qualifies as a Fitter Family."

"Thank you," she replied. "My sister will be grateful to receive this information, and I'm sure she will want verification that we are a Fitter Family."

As she threaded her way through the crowd heading to the harness racing stands, she mused about what had happened. *Of course we are a Fitter Family. Our family goes back in an unbroken line to the arrival of Richard Townsend in Accomac, Virginia in 1670.* She brushed over the fact that he had arrived as an indentured servant and thus may well have come from somewhat "unfit" English stock. But maybe she was justified in ignoring Richard's indentured servant status. Roger Taney, Supreme Court judge from Maryland, who ruled that Dred Scott was not White, asserted that only members of the free, White founding generation are entitled to all rights and privileges stipulated in the US Constitution. There is no question that their great-great-grandfather Zadok Townsend qualified. *How much fitter than that can a family be?*

At the end of a weekend visit in August, Empy told Jessie and Jim that he had accepted a position as clerk at the Du-

Pont Company. He was thrilled at the prospect of working at company headquarters in the recently constructed magnificent DuPont building set right on Caesar Rodney Square in the heart of downtown Wilmington. This would be his last visit to Snow Hill for some time. He was heading north right away to find a room to rent.

"It's been a great summer," Empy said, looking at Jessie. "I've never had such good friends and so many good times in any summer before. Maybe once I get settled, you can visit. Jim and I can show you around Wilmington. After being in school there, we both know it pretty well."

"I would love that," Jessie responded, choosing not to remind Empy that she, too, had gone to school in Wilmington. "Maybe we could go to a play at the DuPont Theater. It's in the new building where you work."

"Well, I've never done anything like that before, but I can look into it," he replied sheepishly.

He extended his hand, then abruptly leaned in to give her a quick kiss on the cheek. They both blushed.

"Goodbye for now," he said quietly as he turned to walk to the train station.

"Don't say a word!" she said firmly to Jim.

"Okay; okay," he answered as he went up the front porch steps into the house.

She watched the slender figure turn the corner a block away, trying to ignore the lump in her throat.

1.6

Escape

Ever since Kate's death, Jessie had looked to her sister Helen for advice and affection. Until Jessie's high school graduation in 1909, Helen had been a teacher at Snow Hill High School, but in that year she resigned to go into training as a nurse at Presbyterian Hospital in Philadelphia. Jessie didn't know for sure that Helen had waited to leave Snow Hill High School until her graduation, but she liked to think so.

Helen completed her nurse's training in 1912 and returned home for a few weeks of rest before assuming her duties as a nurse in the operating room of Presbyterian Hospital. She had an exciting story to tell at the dinner table on her first night home. Everyone listened avidly, including Uncle Paul, who had made a habit of joining them for dinner occasionally ever since Father's death. All the children were out of the house now except for occasional visits, so Mother was often alone. And, what's more, Uncle Paul hadn't quite forgiven himself for being unable to save Father.

"Eric, a physician in the operating room at the hospital, acted so responsibly," Helen began. "He put the injured man and boy in the ambulance and rushed them to the emergency room. It was such a tragedy. The ambulance had been rushing Eric to a call when it swept around the corner and struck the man and boy on the motorcycle. They really shouldn't have been stopped there, and of course the ambulance was going fast because Eric was already heading to an emergency."

Clearly engrossed, Jim asked, "What happened to the man and boy?"

"The man was dead," Helen replied. "Eric knew that immediately because he saw that his skull had been crushed, but as a matter of dignity, he took the man with the boy to the hospital. The boy had minor injuries.

"And then both Eric and the ambulance driver were taken to the police station!" she exclaimed. "The ambulance driver was held in jail overnight, but thankfully Eric was released on his own recognizance with a commitment to appear later as a witness. Even though he himself is an emergency room physician, it's still a shock to be a party to such a tragic accident. I know it upset him, although he pretended it didn't."

The family had heard occasional mentions of Dr. Eric Wisehart in letters from Helen over the past few months, but had never heard him referred to in such an informal way—simply *Eric*—until this moment.

"So Dr. Wisehart has become a close friend of yours?" Mother inquired.

"A close colleague, yes," Helen replied. "He has been someone I have come to admire during my training. It will be a privilege to work under him when I return to the hospital."

"I see," Mother replied. Jessie wondered if she saw too. Helen's face had an unusual glow to it—noticeably different from her usual sober, serious demeanor.

A few months later, Jessie was home for a visit and Uncle Paul was again a guest for dinner. Once Mozelle had served

Jessie's mother
The first Helen
Helen Jones Townsend

everyone, he made an announcement: "I have some wonderful news. In August, Dr. Wisehart will be moving to Snow Hill to join me in my practice. He will also buy a share in the Jones Drug Store. I am ecstatic. I have been looking for a young physician with the most up-to-date training to join me for some time."

"Really?!" Mother exclaimed. "How did this come about?"

"Well, after hearing Helen tell the story about Dr. Wiseheart and the ambulance accident, I asked her to introduce us. I visited him at the hospital and talked to his colleagues there. He visited me here and accompanied me on rounds on two different occasions. We have come to an arrangement that suits us both, I believe. It is a great relief to ensure that my patients will have the best of care for another generation."

"Well, Helen has said nothing about this," Mother commented, sounding a bit piqued.

To her surprise, Jessie spoke up.

"Mother, I doubt Helen knew much about this. After all,

Jessie's sister
The second Helen
Helen Townsend Wiseheart Stabler

once she introduced Dr. Wisehart to Uncle Paul, the matter was out of her hands."

To herself, Jessie thought, *Helen is keeping her personal life private. That makes perfect sense to me.*

"Exactly," Uncle Paul replied, casting a grateful glance toward Jessie.

Everyone in the family avoided inviting Mother's interference, even her brothers.

By Christmas of 1913, Eric was a full-fledged participant in the local social scene. Mother opened the house to a Holiday Musicale sponsored by the young women of the Whatcoat Methodist Episcopal Church. Eric attended along with his friend and former colleague Dr. Ralston Wells. Jessie was home, thrilled at the opportunity to sing and play the piano. The next summer, a large group including Eric and Helen and sisters Mary and Eva, chaperoned by Cousin Nell and her husband, traveled to Glen Island, Ontario for a week's stay at a cottage owned by Dr. Wells. Jessie felt a sting of disappointment at not being included with the older crowd.

Home for a rest in October after her appointment as head nurse in the operating room, Helen surprised no one when she announced her engagement to Eric with a wedding date set for June 5, 1915. She would have to give up her promising career to return to live with Eric in Snow Hill, but she expressed no regrets.

Shortly before the ceremony, Helen and Jessie lounged together on the front porch for what would probably be their last chance for sisterly confidences before the wedding. Jessie swallowed hard and began to speak from her heart.

"You are so fortunate, Helen—about to marry an excellent young man of whom Mother approves, and who is situated for life with Uncle Paul. I can't see what the future holds for me."

To her surprise, Helen understood immediately.

"Yes," she said, "I'm sure your life at your job in Onancock is lonely. You're so isolated from friends and family there. And you see Empy so infrequently now that he lives in Wilmington. Have the two of you talked the situation over?"

"I would go there to be with him, but Mother would never permit it. Empy has a good job with the DuPont Company, but his background isn't like Eric's."

"Do you care about that?"

"Not really. I just want a new life. It would be exciting to live in a city like Wilmington and to set up a real home of my own. I'm sure Empy will move up in the world; I'm sure I'll find a social circle there."

"Well, maybe you don't need Mother's permission. You're 22, certainly old enough to make your own decisions. After all, the rest of us have set our own courses."

Exactly, Jessie thought.

"Well, we couldn't get married here in Snow Hill like you. We'd have to go somewhere else."

"That could be arranged. Eric and I could help you."

"You would do that?" Jessie said incredulously. "What about Mother?"

"Mother will forgive eventually, just as she has forgiven Uncle Paul and Eric for arranging a joint practice without involving her. It wasn't her business of course, and your life isn't really her business either. I know the two of you have never been close. Make your own choices."

"Thank you, thank you!" Jessie said as she jumped up to give Helen a quick kiss on her cheek. "I still miss Kate dreadfully, but you have been so kind to me since she died."

"That's what I promised her I would do, and I've come to enjoy it! At this point, I may or may not have children, so looking out for my little sister is extra special."

"One last question," Helen continued. "Are you in love with Empy?"

Jessie blushed. Empy was not Edwin, now a commissioned naval officer, but he was a kind man. Empy was not Eric, a physician with a promising future right here in Snow Hill, but he would build a career in Wilmington. She was sure of that. As Empy's wife, the future might hold promise after all.

"Empy is a wonderful person. I'm going to write to him right away," Jessie replied, as she headed inside abruptly.

At 33, Helen opted for a small wedding with only her family in attendance. She looked lovely in the blue traveling suit she wore as the newlyweds set off in Eric's 25 hp Reo traveling car to visit his parents in Harrisburg and then to journey on to Atlantic City.

In August, two months after their wedding, Helen and Eric motored to Onancock to bring Jessie home for one of her periodic visits. This time, Jessie would not be returning.

"I have an exciting new position in a big city," she had told Attorney Powell, her boss and principal in the firm. "I would appreciate it if you would not announce my departure for a few weeks. I would like the family to hear the news from me."

"Ah, a move to Baltimore like so many young people from the Eastern Shore are doing. I can't say that I blame you. Your secret is safe with me," he had replied. Jessie did not correct him.

On August 9, Helen gave a spectacular garden party in honor of Jessie. Although everyone there saw it as the new bride's inaugural social event built around her sister's summer visit, Jessie and Helen knew otherwise. Jessie chatted with Bessie and other friends, wondering how they would greet her the next time they met. Would they be angry that she hid such a big secret, or would they understand?

That evening, she spent an agonizing hour composing a letter to Mother, explaining that she thought the simplest thing was for her and Empy to be married quietly outside of Snow Hill to avoid all awkwardness. She hoped Mother would understand and would still welcome her home for visits.

On August 16, Helen, Eric, and Jessie left for Ocean City where Jessie could enjoy a week of sand and surf before supposedly returning to Onancock. However, on the way, they detoured to Cambridge where Empy was waiting. Helen and Eric were proud to be witnesses to Jessie and Empy's marriage in a local Methodist church. Including the minister, there were five people in the church that day.

Jessie wore the same pale pink organza dress that she had worn when she and Edwin had performed their duet five years before. She was happy to have an occasion to wear it again. Empy looked uncomfortable in his suit, but his smile was radiant as he listened to her recite her vows.

After the ceremony, Helen and Eric motored the newlyweds to their Ocean City destination. The two couples stayed in different hotels to give the new husband and wife some privacy. A week later, Helen and Eric carried them to their new home in Wilmington. As Jessie disembarked from Eric's car, she embraced her sister, whispering "Thank you" in her ear. Helen replied with a tender squeeze.

In mid-September, a wedding announcement appeared in *The Democratic Messenger: Word has just come to us ...,* it began.

Helen had written to Jessie that Mother had intended to place the announcement, but Jessie had scarcely dared to believe her. Evidently, Helen was right—in her way and for her own reasons, Mother had forgiven her. From the outside looking in, all was normal, and Jessie could pick up the threads of her Snow Hill life as Mrs. Milton P. Lewis.

No one outside the family circle need ever know that she had eloped to avoid Mother's cold disapproval of the difference in social class between Empy and her. Judging by Mother's behavior, the transformation of Jessie Townsend into Jessie Lewis was no more remarkable than taking off her hat and coat. That she and Mother never spoke about Jessie's clandestine wedding became just one more grain of sand in the emotional desert of their relationship.

1.7

New Lives Interrupted

Jessie and Empy settled into their home, a rented duplex. After a few months as a full-time homemaker, she began to feel a bit restless. It had been as satisfying as she expected to have a home of her own, although she wished she had spent more time in the kitchen watching Mozelle when she was growing up. Ironing wasn't her strong point either. She had prevailed upon Empy to take his shirts to the laundry so he would look perfect each morning. He had mentioned the expense, but she insisted. Maybe, at some point, they could hire someone. In any case, even though she had much to learn about keeping house, the hours in the middle of the day dragged. She began looking for a job.

For her first step, Jessie visited Mrs. Goldey, principal of Goldey Commercial College, who had been kind to her when she received the unexpected news of her Father's death five years before. Mrs. Goldey was delighted to learn that Jessie was now living in Wilmington.

"You were such a serious and dedicated student," Mrs. Goldey said. "I am sure you will bring those same qualities to your professional work. I will let all our employers know to expect you," she said as she handed Jessie a list. "I suggest that you start with the DuPont Company."

"I wouldn't want to work at the DuPont Company in the same department as my husband," Jessie said, shifting just a bit in her seat.

"Oh no, of course not," Mrs. Goldey replied. "I'm sure they will have a post for you in a different department. After all, it's a very big company, and with the war on in Europe, the demand for ordnance and explosives is very high. The Company needs more people everywhere."

Anyway, Jessie thought, he won't be there forever. With Eric's help, Empy had enrolled in a correspondence course offered by the pharmacy school in Philadelphia, and the plan was, once Empy had his license, they would return to Snow Hill where he would work in the Jones-Wisehart Pharmacy. If she got a job, maybe Empy could study full-time and their dream of returning to Snow Hill would come true even sooner. Maybe Mozelle could come work for her one or two days a week. She smiled at the thought, and then, with a start, realized that Mrs. Goldey had asked her a question.

"You will let me know where you accept a position?" she had asked. "We do like to keep track of our alumnae."

"Oh, yes, of course. Thank you so much for your help," and after a pause, Jessie added, "and for your kindness when my father died. I am sure I didn't thank you at the time."

"You're welcome—on both counts," Mrs. Goldey replied.

A few weeks later, an unexpected letter arrived from Mary. Of Jessie's four sisters, she was least close to Mary. The fourth child of the seven who had survived infancy, Mary got lost in the middle. The oldest, Charlie, had been the one who taught her and Floyd to canoe and shoot, and had covered up for her when she was not where she was supposed to be. Beloved Kate had been her surrogate mother, a role that Helen filled now. Eva, the sister closest in age, had been her companion on social occasions and at school. Jim, closest in age of all, had been annoying as a younger brother, but had become a dear friend once he brought Empy into her life. Mary was just invisible. Jessie could not remember one single instance when she and Mary had shared a personal conversation or marked a milestone together.

However, Mary was also a graduate of Goldey Commercial College and had gone to work at an employment agency in Philadelphia. The letter read:

Dear Jessie,

I have just opened my own employment agency, and I am looking for an office manager. I contacted Mrs. Goldey for a recommendation, and I was quite surprised when she suggested you! I knew, of course, that you and Empy were living in Wilmington, but I did not know you were looking for a job. Could you come to my office at 234 Walnut Street Thursday next to discuss the possibility of working here?

Yours truly,

Mary

What luck! This was perfect. She could easily take the train back and forth. She wrote Mary an immediate reply and walked to post it in time for the next day's mail.

Over the next several months, she and Empy settled into a satisfying routine. She traveled to Philadelphia each morning where she enjoyed being responsible for the smooth running of Mary's office. She and Mary had agreed that she would take a mid-afternoon train home, arriving in time to prepare Empy's supper. He continued to work as a clerk for the DuPont Company, and he was making progress with the pharmacy correspondence course. By spring, he would have a week of vacation, which they planned to spend in Snow Hill—where Empy would apprentice in the Jones-Wisehart Pharmacy. *At last,* she thought on her ride home, *my life is taking shape.*

January 3, 1916 dawned bright and cold. Jessie was looking forward to her first day back in the office since the holiday break. No sooner had she hung up her hat and coat than the phone at her desk rang. The jangling noise startled her, and, for no apparent reason, she felt a sense of foreboding. Answering the phone was a routine part of her job, so why this feeling of dread?

She heard a voice both familiar and strange.

"He's dead, Jessie. Uncle Paul couldn't save him. It was just like Father—healthy in the morning, but dead before the next morning."

At first she did not recognize this voice heavy with grief. And then she did—it was Helen! She was talking about Eric.

"Uncle Paul called it Bright's disease. He died of uremic poisoning. His kidneys slowly shut down, his fever rose, and he became delirious. I have never watched such an agonizing death, and it happened to my beloved Eric. All my nursing skills didn't even keep him comfortable. How could this be?"

Jessie was completely disoriented. Was this Eva calling again to tell her Father had died? No, this was Helen telling her that Eric had died. But they hadn't even been married a year. Why another tragedy? Hadn't her family endured enough?

".... funeral in two days. Please tell Mary and come home." The phone clicked, and Jessie realized Mary was standing in front of her desk.

"What is it?" Mary asked.

"We, we ... have to go home," Jessie stammered.

Four days later, Jessie sat in the living room reading Eric's magnificent obituary in *The Democratic Messenger*. The photo showed a handsome young man in the prime of life. The text described his recent move to Snow Hill, his collaboration with Uncle Paul in their practice as well as the pharmacy. It expressed deep regret that the promise of this new duo would never be fulfilled for Snow Hill. And it listed his wife of five months, Helen Townsend Wisehart, as his survivor. The lump in her throat felt so familiar. How had she ever imagined that it would dissolve?

So many lives interrupted; Helen's most of all. A few days after Eric's obituary appeared, she placed an advertisement that swelled the lump in Jessie's throat:

> *For Sale: An REO sports car with a 25 hp engine. Barely driven; like new. Contact Helen Townsend Wisehart at PO Box 22.*

This was Eric's car—the one he had driven when he and Helen had picked her up in Onancock, when she left her boring job forever; the one they had driven to Cambridge where Empy was waiting for her at the Methodist church; the one that had whisked them away on their honeymoon and then to their new life in Wilmington. But Helen said she would not need a car when she returned to her nursing position in Wilmington. And driving it brought only pain.

Uncle Paul's life was changed too. All his plans for the future dashed, he was weighed down with grief and guilt. He had not saved Father, and now, he had not saved Eric. He decided to sell the pharmacy; he let his practice dwindle over the next few years as his patients died or moved away.

Now that Helen and Eric were not in Snow Hill, and Jessie and Empy would not be located there, Mother accepted her son Charlie's offer to move to Philadelphia with him. She would eventually sell the family home, which suited Jessie—no more wakes in the living room. Empy would continue his pharmacy studies, but who knew where that would lead now. Her dreams of returning to Snow Hill in triumph—as the niece of its prominent physician and the wife of its trusted pharmacist—were crushed.

At least Mary's business was prospering and Jessie still had a job. But the job which had initially been a bridge to a bright future all of a sudden felt like another dead end. It was supposed to have been a stopgap until Empy became established in Eric's pharmacy—but now? Had she escaped drudgery once only to be trapped again? Were her dreams of following in her mother's footsteps to assume a prominent social position in Snow Hill in vain?

1.8

Bitter Champagne

Empy arrived at her bedside with a steaming cup of tea. "I'm surprised the champagne has such an effect on you. You didn't drink that much, and we were home shortly after midnight. Being sick is not the way to start a new year!"

"Maybe it's not the champagne," she replied.

"It's not?" he said, puzzled. "What else could it be?"

"I think we're going to have a baby."

Now it was Empy's turn to look wan and stricken.

"We are?" he said weakly as he sank down on the edge of the bed. "I know you didn't want children until we got more settled."

"Well, things don't always turn out as one hopes. I don't understand why I have to keep learning that lesson," she replied, as memories of the deaths flitted through her mind ... Kate, Father, Eric.

"We will be good parents no matter what," Empy said, repressing the surge of joy welling up in him. He leaned over to give Jessie a kiss, but she turned her head to offer her cheek.

"We will do what is necessary, I'm sure, as we always do. The tea is helping, thank you. I'm going to rest now."

Although he knew he had been dismissed, he hesitated. There was so much he wanted to say. After she slid down under the quilt and turned her back, he walked silently from the room.

A week later at the dinner table, Jessie reported:

"I have seen the doctor. The baby will be born in the fall and he says there is no reason I cannot work into the spring. I have discussed the situation with Mary, and we have agreed that I will leave on Memorial Day. I don't want to be on the train during the hot summer, even though I will go crazy with nothing to do during those last months. I had lunch with Helen; she will help us after I stop working so you can continue the pharmacy course. The sooner you complete that course the better. I will be home with a baby, not working, for a long time."

"Was Helen pleased to hear about the baby?" Empy asked, wishing he had been present when Helen heard the news. "With so much sadness in her life, this might bring her a little happiness."

"Of course she was," Jessie replied tartly. "And she understood at once the strain this puts us under."

"Yes, she has been unfailingly kind to us from the very start," he answered. *Why couldn't Jessie see the good side of things,* he thought, but said nothing more.

"I'm very tired," Jessie said as they finished cleaning up. "I suppose you will stay down here to work on your studies."

"Yes, good night," he said, as he moved to the desk where he kept his pharmacy work. From a secret compartment, he withdrew a small flask and took a swig before settling in.

The birth of the third Helen went smoothly on a lovely October day. Jessie had not wanted to name the child for her mother. She had not really wanted this baby and now that it was here, she had doubts about how to be a mother. Her own mother had certainly not been a good example. However, Empy had insisted that the name honored her sister, not her mother. For once, Jessie acquiesced. She might not be excited about this baby, but Empy certainly was. Why not agree? After all, he had suggested Townsend as the child's middle name, honoring her father.

Empy adored his daughter. He loved the trip to Philadelphia to show her off to Charlie and Mother, and Eva and Mary. He was proud to take the train all the way to the tip of the Delmarva Peninsula to show off the baby to his parents and sister, Tense, and agreed reluctantly, but proudly, for Jessie and the baby to linger in Snow Hill with Uncle Paul and his family. And he asked Jessie to invite Helen to dinner rather than lunch every week so that he could enjoy the sight of Helen holding her namesake. He couldn't help smiling when Helen gave Jessie a few tips from her nurse's perspective. Jessie herself did what she was supposed to do, but Empy couldn't help noticing that she immediately handed the baby over to anyone nearby.

One day in the spring of 1918, Empy arrived home to find Jessie even more agitated than usual.

"This envelope from the Federal Government came for you today," she said as soon as he entered the house. "I know it's addressed to you, but whatever it says affects me too, so I opened it. You have to register for the draft!"

"May I see it please?" he said through clenched teeth.

"I have to report on Saturday, so I will."

"I will go with you and take Helen. I want them to see

that you have a wife and a baby not even a year old! Whatever would I do?"

"If you want to," he said, feeling embarrassed, "although I don't know if that's a place for women and children."

"I wish I had paid more attention to all those women from the International Peace and Freedom League who were marching to keep us out of the war," she continued. "I know it's bad that the Germans keep sinking our ships, but I can't see why our boys should leave their families and go over there!"

"I think the point is that we are fighting to defend ourselves against the tyranny of the Kaiser. Of course I hope I don't have to fight, but if I am sent, I will go. It's my duty."

"I know it's your duty," she said tersely. "I just hope you don't have to abandon us."

"Can we have dinner?"

The dreaded military summons did not arrive; instead a double dose of disaster arrived in a more familiar form.

Jim ... baby brother Jim ... had been diagnosed with tuberculosis shortly after Jessie and Empy had married, but a stay in a sanatorium in Western Maryland had wrought a miraculous cure. He had joined the Coast Guard, completed a romantic tour of duty in golden California, and returned home to marry Marion Baker and set up housekeeping in Philadelphia near Mother and Charlie. Jessie and Empy saw them frequently. Jessie didn't particularly like Marion, but she was eager to play with the baby when they visited, which provided Jessie a welcome respite. Empy and Jim remained good buddies, still going to the races and baseball games as they had always done.

In the spring of 1919, Jessie answered the phone one more time to a voice thick with grief.

"Jessie," Marion said, "Jim's tuberculosis has come raging back, and Helen has arranged for him to go to the sanatorium in the Adirondacks where Kate was treated."

That's a death sentence, Jessie thought. *They didn't save Kate, and they won't save Jim.*

"Please tell Empy. Jim will not be able to meet him at the Phillies game next weekend. Maybe they can catch a late summer game once Jim comes home," she continued in a voice suffused with denial.

Jessie had to bite her tongue to keep from blurting out that there would be no late summer game.

"Of course I'll tell him," she said instead. "He will be distraught to hear that Jim's illness is back, but so grateful to know he is getting care."

Eight weeks later, Marion, with Eva as her companion, traveled with Jim's body back to Snow Hill. The funeral was set for three days hence, and Jessie was determined to go alone.

"Empy, I know he's your good friend, but we can't take Helen. Only one of us can go. I don't want to be the one, but he's my brother so it's my duty. My friend Ruth will take Helen during the day. You can go to work and save your vacation for us for later."

"Jessie, surely one of Uncle Paul's daughters would take charge of Helen while we are there. Jim was not just my good friend; he was my best friend. I cannot bear the thought of missing his funeral."

"You need to keep studying for the pharmacy exam. It's

only a few months away. You can't afford to take time off. And Helen's life would be disrupted by the trip. She needs to remain here with you tucking her into bed as always."

Empy turned away.

The next morning he parted with Jessie and greeted her friend Ruth, when she arrived to pick up Helen. Although Helen had met Ruth on several occasions, she wailed inconsolably when Ruth took her to the car, leaving her father waving forlornly from the porch. At their reunion that evening, she jumped into her father's arms. He couldn't help smiling as he buried his face in her silky hair. The small flask was a particular comfort as he settled down to study after putting Helen to bed.

For her part, as she sat silently on the train with Mother, Charlie, Eva, Mary, and Helen, Jessie was grateful there would not be yet another wake in the living room of the Snow Hill house. This time, the wake would be held at the church, and Uncle Paul would host the supper. She could not repress her feeling of freedom. What a joy to be traveling without an insistent toddler at her side. Two people subtracted from her life in the four years since her wedding, and one unexpectedly (and unenthusiastically) added. Would she ever regain the sense of stability and excitement of a promising future that she had felt before Eric's death?

Two months later, they were all back on the train yet again. Not tuberculosis this time ... A virulent pandemic surging throughout Europe and the United States was the cause of the latest disaster. This time Eva was not with them because she had already accompanied the body of her fiancé, Robert Purnell, back to Snow Hill. He had been the head of

The Peddie School in New Jersey, where so many Snow Hill boys prepared for the Naval Academy. Robert himself had been a student there and had served with distinction in the Navy before beginning his career at Peddie. Eva was now in charge of the Peddie infirmary, and the family had smiled as a romantic relationship had developed between them as it had years before between Helen and Eric. This time, the family had dared hope there would be years of happiness.

Over the past month, Peddie had seen several cases of the Spanish Flu among the students and the teachers; Helen had urged Eva to wear a mask at all times and to insist that anyone coming to the infirmary do the same. Helen knew Robert as well, and she had written to him urging that he dismiss the school for the rest of the term, pointing out that Eva was in mortal danger as she cared for sick students until transportation home could be arranged. Ironically, it was Robert who had been in mortal danger, and his death had prompted the closure of The Peddie School for at least the rest of the term. All students were sent home. With luck, the pandemic would subside, and the Board of Trustees could find a new head so Peddie could reopen in the new year. With luck, Eva would have a job to return to if she could bear to return to the campus where Robert's absence would be palpable.

On this train trip, Jessie was just numb. No exhilarating feelings of freedom. No worries about the future. No feelings of sympathy for Eva, whose life had been upturned just as Helen's had been ... just an enveloping fog.

1.9

REVIVED

On a spring day in 1920, once again Empy found Jessie with an open letter in her hand when he returned home. Even though this time she was grinning from ear to ear, he felt no less annoyed. Why could she not let him open his own mail?

"I know you think I shouldn't have opened this letter, but I was so sure it was good news that I just couldn't resist!" she said with a lilt in her voice that had been missing for a very long time. He melted in spite of himself.

"You passed!" she exclaimed. "And you are to go to a meeting of the Delaware State Pharmacy Board at the Hotel DuPont in two weeks to receive your license as an Assistant Pharmacist. I am so proud of you for all your hard work. I wish Father had known you. He would be proud of you too!"

"Thank you," he said. "I would have liked to have known your father. I know how much you loved him. May I see the letter?"

And there it was: *"Dear Mr. Lewis, We write to congratulate you ..."* He had not gotten much further than that when Jessie wrapped him in a bear hug, and he melted again. Such a long time since they had embraced with joy ...

Two weeks later, as Jessie waited impatiently for Empy to

return home from the Pharmacy Board meeting, she could not help but muse on the contrast between this day and so many awful days in the recent past. How much things had changed for the better since 1918 when Empy had registered for the draft! The war was over—and President Wilson had promised that we would never have another one. The pandemic was over; no one even wore a mask anymore. Empy would soon have a real profession—one much more impressive than just being a clerk at the DuPont Company. The sudden deaths of Eric and Robert and the lingering deaths of Kate and Jim had taught her that tragedy could envelop her at any moment; nevertheless, she actually felt happy.

Barely a day later, Jessie sat at her desk composing a letter to Uncle Paul. Although he had threatened to sell his pharmacy in Snow Hill after Eric's untimely death destroyed their plans, years later he still owned it—and it was flourishing. She wrote:

> *Dear Uncle Paul,*
>
> *I write with glorious news. Empy has received his pharmacy license! While I know that Eric's death completely upended all your plans, Empy now has the professional certificate that would have qualified him to take his place in the Snow Hill pharmacy as a member of the Jones/Wiseheart team. You have been such a stalwart supporter of all of us as we have faced tragedy after tragedy. I am hoping you might see your way to support us again, but this time in pursuit of a positive goal. Do you have any connections that might find Empy a place in a pharmacy here in Wilmington?*
>
> *With eternal gratitude,*
>
> *Jessie*

That evening after Empy had tucked Little Helen into bed, he joined Jessie in the parlor.

"I have made a list of pharmacies in the city," he said, "and a list of their proprietors. I met several of them at the Board meeting. I plan to write each of them to inquire after a place."

"Yes, that's a good idea," Jessie replied, "but I'm hoping Uncle Paul will make all that unnecessary. I posted a letter today asking about his connections in the city. I'm confident it will bear fruit."

Empy was silent, struggling to suppress his emotions.

After a long pause, he said stiffly, "Jessie, I know you mean well, but I am aggrieved you would write such a letter without discussing it with me. After all, this is about my career, and I feel strongly that I should be the one charting its course. This action of yours is just as objectionable as your practice of opening my mail."

"Empy, sometimes I don't understand you at all. You must know that I have only your best interests at heart; secondly, it's not just your career—it's my life too. I have every right to be involved."

"I don't deny that you have a right to be involved; in fact, I yearn for discussions about our future. But I do deny your right to act unilaterally, even when the idea is a good one," he concluded lamely.

"Fooey," she said. "I'm going to bed."

Once her footsteps faded, he went to the desk to retrieve his small flask. Returning to his chair, he took a long pull and laid his head back. Why, oh why, did their conversations always go like this? He felt so ground down. Nothing he said prompted her to modify her behavior in the slightest; she was becoming a piece of sandpaper that rubbed him raw.

A month later a telegram arrived:

> *Have news. Visiting your mother and sisters in Philly. Will stop in Wilmington on return trip Thursday week. Paul*

The telegram was addressed to her, which was a relief. Empy would have no grounds for complaint when she showed it to him.

"I heard from Uncle Paul," she announced at dinner. "He will visit us Thursday week and he has news."

"Wonderful!" he exclaimed. "Did he give any details?"

"No details, so we'll just have to bide our time. But it is encouraging."

"Very!" Empy agreed.

Uncle Paul's news exceeded their expectations. He had purchased a pharmacy which he hoped Empy would manage. The arrangements would allow Empy to build up an ownership percentage so that one day the store would be his. He would begin on the first of September.

When Uncle Paul visited, Empy was quick to express his gratitude.

"I am speechless," Empy said as Paul outlined the framework of the deal. "I do not know how to thank you appropriately."

"Just make a success of it." Paul smiled. "That will be thanks enough."

Jessie added, "Uncle Paul, once again we see why you are Mother's favorite brother. You have been a bona fide member of our family ever since Father died. I don't know how we would have managed without you."

"It has been my privilege," he replied, turning to Empy. "I have brought a contract which we should go over carefully."

"Jessie," Empy said immediately, "maybe you can put Helen to bed tonight while Paul and I work at my desk?"

She started to object—didn't this contract affect her?—but Paul stopped her with one word.

"Excellent," he said, and she knew she had been put in her place.

In October, when Helen joined them for dinner to celebrate Little Helen's third birthday, a brand new topic arose. Who would they vote for? All the women Jessie knew, both family and friends, were eagerly anticipating the first presidential election ever when women from all over the country could vote. Jessie's friend, Ruth Cann, had been trying to persuade her to vote for Warren Harding, the Republican.

"Ruth really thinks we should vote for Warren Harding," Jessie said. "He will lead us in a return to normalcy."

"I don't know," Helen spoke up. "Our family has always been Democrats."

"Yes, but the economy is in terrible shape," Jessie countered. "There are all those strikes of steelworkers and mineworkers, and the race riot in Chicago, and revolution in Europe. And why should we join the League of Nations and get entangled yet again in the affairs of foreign countries? All of this under a Democratic president!"

"Remember Uncle Robley," Helen continued. "He was elected state attorney for Worcester County three times on the Democratic ticket, and when he was elected to the House of Delegates, he sponsored the law that turned Worcester County dry. That's an achievement I have always admired! Then he was appointed to the Circuit Court and served as a highly respected judge for nine years before he died. How could we turn away from his legacy?"

Jessie wasn't giving up. "And anyway, President Wilson has had a stroke and won't be able to help the League get started, so who knows what will happen to it? And last but not least, Teddy's sister, Corrine, is urging all women to support the Republican. I thought Teddy was a wonderful president and I wish he hadn't died last year. If he had run again, I would vote Republican for sure!"

Helen wasn't giving up either. "Mother and Uncle Paul would be appalled to think that we would vote against the party of their brother, Judge Robley Jones. Father was a lifelong Democrat too."

Empy, who had been quiet so far, spoke up with animation. "Well, I am not a supporter of temperance so that argument doesn't persuade me to vote Democrat. And I cannot forget that the Republicans are the party of Lincoln. I hail from Virginia, and I cannot vote for a party that destroyed our Southern way of life. I'll be voting for James Cox. And Teddy's cousin, Franklin, is his vice-presidential candidate. So not all Roosevelts are Republican."

"I know our whole family votes Democrat," Jessie said, "but I want to think for myself. I really like the notion of a return to normalcy. I want the drug store to be a success, and I think Mr. Harding will probably do a better job for businesses like ours."

Jessie was vindicated. Warren Harding won in a landslide,

even carrying Tennessee, the first Confederate state to vote Republican since Reconstruction. She could not help but remember the recent evening when Uncle Paul had dismissed her out of hand. He had been wrong to do that, and, through the election results, she had received affirmation of her capable, independent mind. She was careful not to gloat, however. The first time Helen came for dinner after the election, no one breathed a word about it.

1.10

GLORY DAYS

Little Helen was ready. Her dress was crisply ironed, her shoes polished, her hair brushed and tied back with a smart ribbon. She seemed stoic about the prospect of her first day in first grade. Jessie was elated, although she tried to conceal her feelings. She and Empy had agreed that he would walk Little Helen to school on his way to the pharmacy, and that she would meet their daughter at the end of the day to walk her home. As soon as they were out the door, Jessie would be blessed with six hours of freedom! And she had plans.

"She's ready," Jessie called up the stairs.

"I'm coming," Empy replied as he headed down.

"Are you ready for your big day?" he said with a grin as he took Little Helen's hand. "Give your mother a kiss," he urged. Jessie bent down stiffly to receive a peck on her cheek.

Turning to Jessie he said, "Wish her well."

"I know you'll have a wonderful day," Jessie replied as she held the front door open wide.

Several hours later, it was Jessie's turn to grin as she opened the front door to welcome her friend Ruth Cann. Now that Jessie was free, they had agreed to weekly lunches, the first one at Jessie's house, then alternating houses after that.

As they settled into egg salad sandwiches, sliced fresh peaches, and iced tea, Ruth said, "I have a surprise for you, and I have been waiting for this special day to tell you. I am sponsoring you for membership in the Washington Heights Century Club!"

Jessie was speechless. She had been fortifying herself to ask Ruth for that very thing, but Ruth had done it on her own initiative. There was nothing on earth that she desired more. The first Century Club had been founded in Seattle in 1891 by Carrie Chapman Catt as a vehicle for advancing women's suffrage. The name signified the suffragettes' belief that the century of the 1800s was dedicated to the advancement of women. They had been off by two decades, but now that the vote had been safely secured for three years, the century clubs had evolved into a highly prized, but somewhat exclusive, site of women's social activity.

"Ruth, I cannot thank you enough. Ever since I attended their events as your guest, I have wanted to be a member. This is a dream come true."

"And ever since I realized how wonderful you are at performing—singing, playing the piano, dramatic readings—I've known you would be a great addition to our group. And you have business experience so I'm sure you will contribute to running the club too. I'm so glad you are pleased!" Ruth replied. "Now we'll have to get you prepared for your interview."

At dinner that night, Empy tried to stay focused on Little Helen. "Tell us about your day," he prodded her. "Did you meet some new little girls? Did you show the teacher that you can read?"

Little Helen answered enthusiastically. "I met a girl named Elva. She lives near our house. And the teacher asked us our letters, and if we knew them. Then she asked us to read. She said 'Very good' to me when I could read Twinkle, Twinkle Little Star ...,"

Jessie broke in. "I have news too," she announced proudly. "Ruth is sponsoring me to the Washington Heights Century Club! Isn't that wonderful?"

Empy sighed inwardly. Out loud, he said, "Congratulations. I know that is something you will enjoy."

"Well, it's not a fait accompli yet," Jessie continued. "I have to prepare for my interview ...,"

Empy glanced at Helen, who said nothing more as her mother continued to describe all that was required for the interview. He became quiet too. Jessie seemed not to notice.

At their luncheon several months later, Jessie and Ruth were discussing a problem. As Ruth had expected and Jessie had hoped, Jessie had been swept into the main current of club activities. She found it an interruption to fetch Helen from school each day, never mind keeping up with her housework. She was determined not to let her standards slip—the immaculate condition of her home had been her main source of pride since she stopped working when Helen was born. She and Ruth agreed that she needed a maid. After all, hadn't her mother had help all her life? And yes, she had eight children while Jessie had only one, but the Century Club had not been an option for her mother. Modern life had its own set of demands. Ruth helped her figure out a strategy for convincing Empy, and she walked home rehearsing her speech. She would make her presentation that very evening.

"Empy, I have been asked to be in charge of the games room for the Halloween event at the Club, but I did not accept."

He took the bait as she knew he would. "Why not?" he replied. "That's something you would enjoy and be good at."

"Well, it's a lot of work. I have to plan the games, shop for the supplies, set up the room before the event, and clean up afterward. All that will take me away from the household; I can't let you and Helen down."

"We can make do with a bit less of your attention for a period of time," he said.

"I would hate to see the condition of our home deteriorate. And if I'm successful at this, I will be asked to do other things, so this may not be only a short period when I am pulled away. I think we need a permanent solution. Maybe it's time to hire help. After all, the pharmacy is doing so well ...," she trailed off.

Midway through her speech, Empy knew he had been trapped. Would he ever see four steps ahead so that he could avoid these situations? Not that he objected to a maid, but he hated the way she manipulated him so easily. Nonetheless, he would agree graciously to conceal his anger.

"Yes, I think we could afford someone now. Maybe her hours could include time when Helen is home. She might enjoy having someone new in the house."

"Yes, that's a good idea. Ruth will help me find someone. I was going to place an advertisement in the *News Journal,* but Ruth reminded me that many Coloreds can't read. She will ask her maid to inquire at her church."

He should have known that Ruth was in on the plot. But if

the person turned out to be a friend to his daughter, he would completely forgive Jessie for the subterfuge. He knew that Helen and Jessie would never be close, and he worried about the cold temperature in the house during the afternoon hours before he got home. He was sure Helen was very lonely.

He was gratified by Jessie's report at dinner a few weeks later.

"Ada seems to be working out just fine. The clothes she irons come out beautifully, and I really don't have to check up on her cleaning work. I do just so she won't get the idea she can slack off. And best of all, Helen seems to like her. She does her lessons in the kitchen where Ada irons, or plays under the dining room table while Ada bustles around with the duster."

"And Ada came just in time," she rattled on. "I was even busier with preparations for the Halloween event at the club than I expected! I was a little worried about bobbing for apples, but we loved bobbing in Snow Hill, and it was popular here too. The game of charades was the biggest hit, though. Next year I will make even more cards!"

"Wonderful," Empy replied. "I certainly am enjoying my crisply ironed shirts." Turning to Helen, he asked, "Do you like having Ada in the house?"

"Yes! She has a snack for me when I get home from school, and she sings while she works, and she makes me laugh."

"Well, we're all happy. Thank you, Ada," he said.

"And thank you, Ruth, for helping us find her," Jessie added.

"And thank you, Ruth," Empy repeated, striving to keep a rueful tone from his voice.

Four years later on a spring morning in 1927, Jessie was standing nervously in front of the full-length mirror in her bedroom. Ada was struggling to pin a corsage to her dress.

"Hurry up, Ada," Jessie urged. "The photographer will be here any minute!"

"Land's sake alive, Miss Jessie," Ada replied. "If you don't hold still, I'm gonna stick this pin right through you. You're wiggling worse than Miss Helen does when I pin a hem!"

"Alright, alright," Jessie answered as she held herself rigidly.

How could she not wiggle at the prospect of being photographed for the *Wilmington News Journal*? This picture would be featured in the Sunday Society section atop an article proclaiming her appearance in the title role of the Century Club production of *Sophronia*. First published in 1906 about life at a women's college, this was the play's debut in Wilmington.

Ada successfully secured the luscious corsage to her left shoulder. "My, my, you do look mighty fine!" Ada declared as she stepped back to admire the effect.

Examining herself in the mirror, Jessie had to agree. Her dark hair was stylishly short and curly, framing her face and drawing attention to its perfect oval shape. Her wavy bangs drew attention to her round eyes—her best feature, she thought. The corsage enhanced the effect of the long string of beads around her neck.

"Thank you. I'll wait here until the photographer arrives."

As she waited anxiously for the door knocker downstairs to sound, she daydreamed. Secretly she wished that she really was Sophronia. Sophronia's parents had scrimped and saved so that she could go east to college all the way from Iowa.

IN PLAY TITLE ROLE

—Photo by Ells Studio.

MRS MILTON P. LEWIS

With great interest the members and friends of the Washington Heights Century Club are awaiting the presentation of the comedy, "Sophronia's Wedding," to be given on Friday evening in the Wilmington New Century Club by the Washington Heights Century Club Dramatic League. The play is the first production of the league. Mrs. Milton P. Lewis will be seen in the title role of "Sophronia." Mrs. Lewis is a member of the board of directors of the club. This year she has served as chairman of the hospitality committee. She lives at 10 West Nineteenth street.

Jessie in a promotional photo for the Century Club performance of Sophronia *in which she played the title role*

This appeared in the Evening Journal, *Wilmington, DE, May, 4, 1927*
Image is in the public domain

Jessie's parents hadn't, and then Father died. Her thoughts drifted to that party in Snow Hill to celebrate her crowd departing for college—except her. Instead she went away to work. She didn't think she would ever recover from the disappointment, even though it was more than fifteen years ago. She kept telling herself not to be bitter. No one knew Father would die. Why did he?

Where was that photographer? If he didn't hurry up, it might be time to go meet Helen at school. How annoying. Helen will be ten next year. It's time for her to walk by herself.

Jessie sank back into her daydreams. She acknowledged that she would rather have been one of the other girls in the play—Madeleine or Ethel, who always knew they were going to college and, when they got there, they were in the middle of the social whirl—just where she knew she belonged! Sophronia was an outcast, and even though she got the boy in the end, Jessie would never have traded four years of being a bookworm and an outcast just to get the boy.

A thump, thump at the door announced the photographer's arrival. Sophronia smiled and rose to greet him.

1.10

Up and Down

"Miss Jessie," Ada called, "you best hurry up now. Empy and Miss Helen are ready. You'll be late."

Jessie was startled. Sophronia had been staring back at her from the full-length mirror, and it took a moment for Jessie to emerge. "Ah, yes," she murmured quietly, "today, I am Tense's matron of honor. That's why I am wearing a gorgeous blue silk dress, silver stockings, and black satin shoes."

Hortense Lewis, or Tense as she was known in the family, was Empy's only sibling. A few years earlier, when she had moved to Philadelphia where Mother now lived, she and Empy had begun to see Tense more frequently. Once she met Steele, Tense's fiancé, the two couples became fast friends. Tense had asked Empy to walk her down the aisle, and Little Helen was to be the flower girl; everyone in the family had a part to play.

Jessie knew she should be full of excitement on this special day, but instead she felt dread. Helen would be there, but Eric would not. Marion would be there, but Jim would not. And Kate would not. And Father would not. Why did the absences always press in on her at family celebrations? Couldn't she focus on those who would be present?

Tense herself was an antidote to Jessie's gloomy mood. Always ebullient, on this day she was especially radiant walking down the aisle on Empy's arm. Her caramel-colored dress was the perfect complement to her shining copper-colored hair—and her bouquet of yellow chrysanthemums enhanced the overall effect. Her negative mood notwithstanding, Jessie smiled as Tense approached the altar.

At the wedding dinner following the ceremony, Little Helen suddenly caught her attention. Steele had asked the ten-year-old to dance, and there she was, moving gracefully in response to his gentle guidance. *My heavens, my daughter is growing into a beauty! How did I not notice*? She smiled again. *This is a joyous occasion after all.* As she turned to Empy to express her happiness, he slipped a small silver flask into his pocket.

◆ ◆ ◆

Usually Jessie was immensely pleased when she or Empy appeared in the *Wilmington News Journal*, but today was a major exception. *The Journal* had published an article about a bad check cashed at Empy's store. Evidently he had cashed a check for a man he hardly knew, but the bank rejected it! She was mortified. Why wasn't Empy suspicious? He was just too nice sometimes.

Thankfully, two days later, a second article appeared about the check; Mr. Anderson, the man whose check Empy cashed, was duped too. Evidently, he had accepted the check for $15 from a man he knew in exchange for cash, and then cashed the check in Empy's store. The article says that "Mr. Anderson is now on the trail of the other man." Jessie felt this made Empy look less gullible, and she felt slightly less embarrassed, but they were still out $15!

◆ ◆ ◆

By 1932, the Depression had everyone in its iron grip. Most evenings, dinner was a glum affair with little positive news, but one evening that summer, Empy surprised her.

"I have good news for a change. The pharmacy has been voted a postal substation. We won't make much money from it, but it should increase foot traffic—which will help us."

"That's wonderful! Why didn't you tell me that you had applied?"

"Well, I was not sure we would be accepted, and I didn't want to disappoint you. I know how the hard times are affecting you, and I didn't want to add to your burden."

"Well, you know I much prefer to be in the know; anyway, this is very good news. I wish Helen was here to hear it. I will write to her this evening."

"I was planning on doing that," Empy said.

He knew that his daughter would be cheered by the news. She detested her month-long isolation at his parents' home in Hallwood at the remote tip of the Delmarva Peninsula. Ever since Helen was twelve, Jessie had insisted that she spend a month every summer in Hallwood, arguing that Helen should know her relatives on both sides of the family. Grandmother Helen and the aunts lived just a half-hour train ride away in Philadelphia, but Hallwood was at the end of the world. Consequently, there were no visits there during the school year. Although they had never confided in one another, both Helen and Empy knew that Jessie's real motivation for her exile was much more self-serving. She luxuriated in the month of her "vacation from motherhood" when she could focus single-mindedly on the people and activities she enjoyed.

"No need. I'll do it," Jessie replied.

Empy nodded, but continued to compose his letter mentally.

◆ ◆ ◆

About a year later, another appalling article appeared in *The Journal.* Yet again, Empy had not forewarned her. As soon as he walked in the front door, Jessie demanded an explanation.

"Why didn't you tell me that Tommy Murphy was scammed? Have we really lost $27?"

Slowly and deliberately, Empy took off his coat. He looked around for Helen.

"I fully intended to tell both you and Helen the complete story, but that meant waiting until I heard back from the police, which I did today. Why don't you put dinner on the table, and I will tell you both at once."

He walked upstairs to freshen up as he did every evening. Jessie sputtered, but turned toward the kitchen.

Once they were all seated at the dinner table, he told them an astonishing story:

"Yesterday I gave Tommy $27 to buy stamps for the postal station. He was on his way back to the store when a man approached him with a plea to run an urgent errand for him. Tommy hesitated, but the man appeared desperate so he agreed. The man asked if Tommy had anything the man could hold as security while he ran the errand. Tommy gave him the stamps and then headed to Caesar Rodney Square as the man directed him. But halfway there, Tommy had second thoughts and ran back to the spot where he had met the man. Of course he was gone. Tommy was in tears when he returned to the store. I don't blame Tommy; he's only 17 and has been such a good helper. The police are investigating."

Jessie was silent, but Helen spoke up.

"I don't blame Tommy either," she said. "I see him in school often and sometimes he talks to me about how proud he is to work for you. He just made a mistake."

"I guess that's true," Jessie said, "but I don't understand how the two of you can take the loss of the stamps so calmly. Times just keep getting harder and harder, and we still have to replace the stamps. I only hope President Roosevelt is planning a miracle."

Empy and Helen exchanged glances. They finished their meal in silence.

1.12

No More Little Helen

On a bright fall afternoon in 1934, Helen burst through the front door trailed by her two best friends, Elva and Louise. Jessie was ready to chastise her for being over an hour late, but she didn't get the chance.

"Mother!" Helen exclaimed. "You'll never guess what happened at Empy's store today!"

In her wildest dreams, Jessie could not imagine anything happening at Empy's store that would evoke such excitement. She knew Helen and her friends often congregated at the soda fountain after school, but surely a Cherry Coke was not the explanation.

"I have no idea, but I certainly hope it explains why you are home so late," Jessie replied.

Helen ignored the rebuke and plunged into her story.

"A photographer who is shooting photographs for Coca-Cola advertisements appeared. He asked to take our picture drinking from Coke glasses. He took dozens of them from all different angles and with different filters and light. By the time he finished, there was quite a crowd in the store. You should have been there."

Been there? she thought. *Little chance of that.* She hadn't been in the store for at least a year.

"As he packed up," Helen continued, "he said that we had been terrific models and that he was sure *The Saturday Evening Post* would run one of the photos. Evidently they have a Coke ad in every issue. Wouldn't that be unbelievable?!"

Not really, Jessie thought. Helen had fulfilled the promise of beauty that Jessie had first noticed at Tense's wedding, and at 17 she was stunning.

"Well, well," she said. "That was certainly something special, and I am sure the photographer was right. After all, you—and your friends—are very attractive young ladies. Will he notify you when the photo appears?"

"He took Empy's card and said he would send a copy of the photo to the store along with a copy of the issue in which it appears. Probably sometime next spring, but that's a long time to wait!"

"Well, I'm sure they plan issues far ahead so several months from now makes sense."

"I'm going to walk home with Elva and Louise. We have so much to talk about. I'll be home soon." And she was out the door before Jessie could remind her that dinner would be on the table in a half hour.

After Helen went to her room to do homework, Jessie and Empy sat silently in the living room. Jessie clenched her jaw while Empy tapped his foot.

"Go ahead and ask me," he said. "I'm surprised you didn't ask at dinner."

"I didn't want to put a damper on Helen's excitement," Jessie replied. "And we've agreed to keep our differences private."

"Well, that was unusually thoughtful of you. I'm glad you kept our agreement. We're alone now, so get it off your chest."

Helen #3, center, in the Coke ad which appeared in The Saturday Evening Post *and* The National Geographic

This image is used for illustrative purposes only and is not intended to be representative of the characters or events in this book. It is reproduced with permission from The Coca-Cola Company.

"You had to have known that the photographer was coming, but you didn't tell me, and you should have," she said bitterly.

"Yes," he replied. "They called about a month ago saying they were looking for a drug store with a soda fountain and a teenage clientele. We fit their specifications perfectly. About two weeks ago, they came for a tour and confirmed that our fountain was exactly what they were looking for—right down to our Coke glasses. We set today as the date after I told them that Helen and her friends were here every Wednesday without fail, but I didn't tell her or you."

"Why not?"

"Actually the photographer asked me not to tell her. He wanted to encounter her and her friends in their customary setting without the primping or nervousness that would have occurred if they were expecting him. I didn't tell you because I couldn't trust you not to tell her. And it worked out just as the photographer hoped. The girls were astonished, flattered, and exuberant. Just wait until you see the photograph. They are glowing."

Jessie rose and walked upstairs to their bedroom; a pit settled in her stomach.

Empy picked up his copy of *The Pharmacy Journal.* When he was sure she was not returning, he retrieved the silver flask from the desk.

In early June, Empy arrived home carrying an envelope. Although it was addressed to him, he had not opened it.

"Here," he said to Helen. "Although this is addressed to me, it's really for you."

Helen immediately noticed the return address—Stuart Photography Studios. She had almost given up, but here it was. Inside was a photograph of three girls smiling gaily at a soda fountain. Two of them were sipping from Coke glasses, but the one in the center gazed confidently forward with a radiant smile.

"Empy, this is my graduation present, and there's nothing I would have wanted more. I know you must have arranged the whole thing. Thank you so much. It was such fun." And she stepped forward to give her father a big hug.

Slightly embarrassed, Empy replied, "Oh, you never know. Maybe next year a photographer will turn up at Goldey-Beacom Business College next year looking for models using Olivetti typewriters!"

They both laughed.

"Now go show your mother."

Helen walked slowly toward the kitchen.

Unbeknownst to Helen, thousands of miles away, a promising young chemist was graduating from Colorado College. While she attended Goldey-Beacom Business School following in her parents' footsteps, he pursued a PhD at Ohio State. While he was completing his dissertation, she worked in the steno pool of the DuPont Company in downtown Wilmington. He graduated, and simultaneously she transferred to a job at the Experimental Station, the site of the DuPont Company's basic research. In this job, she helped orient new hires by overseeing their enrollment in the health and pension plans and gave them tours of the common rooms of the huge complex like the cafeteria, library, and locker rooms.

The atmosphere at the Experimental Station was electric. Ever since Neville Chamberlain had signed away the Sudetenland to the Germans, the pace of hiring had accelerated. Although Jessie was confident that the country would stay out of any war because Woodrow Wilson had promised that the last war had been the war to end all wars, Helen could tell that no one at the Experimental Station believed that. The stream of engineers, physicists, and chemists parading past her desk was continuous. It seemed like Uncle Dupie (as insiders called the DuPont Company) was vacuuming up every newly credentialed scientist in the country. And with today's news that Germany had invaded Poland, she had no doubt that the hiring would continue apace.

On a sweltering late summer day, at precisely 8:15 a.m., the door opened to admit today's new arrival.

"Good morning. I am Richard Brooks. You must be Miss Lewis. I was instructed to begin my day here."

She stood up and extended her hand. "Yes, I am expecting you," she replied as she held his gaze. "Welcome to the DuPont Company, Dr. Brooks. Let's go into the conference room where I have a folder of materials and forms that will enroll you in the benefit plans. After that, we'll take a tour which will end in your laboratory where Dr. Bell will take you under his wing for the rest of the day."

"Yes, thank you," he replied. "I look forward to reconnecting with Dr. Bell. I met him when he visited Ohio State.

At dinner that night, both Jessie and Empy were glum. Empy was the first to share his thoughts.

"Britain and France will surely declare war on Germany in the next day or two. And the pressure for the United States to follow suit will become enormous."

"Yes, but France has the Maginot Line, which is impenetrable," Jessie responded, "and the English Channel is a huge barrier to invading armies."

"That was before airplanes. No little water ditch will protect England from air attack."

"Well, the French will stop them, and, in any case, President Roosevelt has promised not to entangle us in European problems."

This was more or less the same conversation her parents had been having for a year, and the continuous repetition of their disagreement irritated Helen more and more.

"Let me tell you about my day," she interrupted. "I welcomed another new scientist. This one is an organic chemist from Ohio State, but he grew up in Colorado. He was telling me about Pikes Peak and the cog train that takes you right to the top—over 5000 feet high! Can you imagine?"

"Well," Jessie said, "it appears that you talked about a lot more than organic chemistry."

"Mother," Helen protested, "making small talk is part of my job! They are always nervous on their first day, and I help them feel at ease."

◆ ◆ ◆

Jessie continued to participate in activities at the Century Club. Contract bridge was the latest craze, and she and her friend Lura Wood had won the latest tournament. Empy was learning to play bridge too and was becoming quite good at it.

Lura had a summer home in Bethany Beach, Delaware, barely a block from the ocean. The beach was wide and covered in fine sand just like that at Ocean City. Jessie and Empy had spent several weekends there with Lura and her husband Phil. Lura had twin daughters about Helen's age, and several times Helen had joined them at Lura's cottage. Even though the drive was over two hours—longer if the drawbridge over the Indian River Inlet was up—everyone loved it. The women loved the beach and enjoyed plunging under the waves at high tide. At low tide, they would stand in shallow, warm tidal pools, allowing their feet to sink into the wet, soft sand. Empy was delighted to discover that Phil liked horse racing as much as he did, and the two of them headed to the Ocean Downs harness track whenever possible. On evenings when the horses were not running, the four of them walked the boardwalk for an ice cream cone, and then sat on a bench watching the moon rise over the ocean as they licked their cones. On rainy evenings they played bridge, enjoying cigarettes and drinks. What a pleasure that Prohibition had been repealed!

Jessie was swept by nostalgia during these weekends, remembering Empy and Jim heading to Ocean Downs, and remembering their honeymoon in Ocean City— with Helen and Eric discreetly staying out of their sight. She found herself leaning against Empy as they sat on their bench. He responded by putting his arm around her shoulders.

Neither Jessie nor Empy was surprised a few months later when Helen announced that she had invited her organic chemist colleague for dinner. She had been out more and more—with groups of friends from work, she said. She had told her parents about a favorite place where they whirled away the night dancing to Glenn Miller, Count Basie, and Louis Armstrong.

"I've invited Dick Brooks for dinner on Friday night. I hope that's all right. He's the chemist from Colorado I mentioned before."

Jessie and Empy exchanged glances and tried not to smile. No doubt Dick Brooks had been among the group that enjoyed dancing to the swing bands.

"Yes, that's fine," Jessie replied. "I'll see if Ada can help out that evening so I won't have to spend time in the kitchen."

"Yes, that's a good idea, but Dick will make the drinks. He likes a very dry martini with an olive. I know we don't have gin or vermouth so I will buy those. Would either of you like a special cocktail?"

"Why, yes," Empy replied. "We have been enjoying Old Fashioneds with Lura and Phil. Can Dick make those?"

"Oh, yes," Helen replied. "He's a genius at cocktails. He

even makes his own bitters and simple syrup! I'll check with him and make sure we have all the ingredients for Old Fashioneds."

"And Dick is an excellent bridge player," she continued. "We play at lunch sometimes, or sometimes a foursome gathers over the weekend. Depending on how the evening goes, we could play if you like."

"Well," Jessie responded. "Dick sounds like a man of many talents."

"Oh, yes. He has been asked to work with the team trying to formulate synthetic rubber. That's such a high priority because if Japan enters the war and cuts off access to the rubber plantations in Burma ...,"

Helen's voice trailed off as she noticed the scowl crossing her mother's face. She stood up abruptly.

"I promised Elva I would come over this evening. Let me clear the table; then I have to run."

Friday evening arrived, and the doorbell rang promptly at 6. Jessie answered it to find herself facing a most handsome young man neatly dressed in a smart suit. Late twenties, she judged, with a winning smile.

"Welcome."

"Mrs. Lewis," he replied. I'm so pleased to meet you. And these are for you. I hope they are a promise of an early spring."

"Daffodils! Ours are just poking through the ground. What a treat to have some in bloom!"

She could feel Helen hovering in the background.

"I'll take these to Ada. Why don't you introduce Dr. Brooks to your father?"

Empy rose from his chair, extending his hand.

"Empy, this is Dick Brooks."

"How do you do, sir?" Dick replied, shaking Empy's hand firmly.

Empy noticed that Dick did not look the least bit surprised when Helen addressed him as Empy. He wondered what else Helen had told him about the family.

"I've told Empy and Mother that you make delicious cocktails, Dick. Let me show you to the sideboard in the dining room. And I'd like to introduce you to Ada, who has worked for our family since I was a little girl. She is roasting what will be the juiciest roast beef you've ever eaten. And she's making popovers!"

"Popovers? What are those?" Dick asked as he followed Helen toward the delicious aromas wafting toward them from the kitchen.

"Ada, please meet Dr. Brooks."

"Are you the creator of all these wonderful smells?" Dick asked with a twinkle in his eye. "I surely picked the right place for dinner tonight."

Ada chuckled. "Well, Dr. Brooks, you better wait and see how it tastes before you say that!"

Dick returned to the living room carrying a tray bearing two Old Fashioneds appropriately garnished with orange slices and maraschino cherries, and two Martinis, each with an olive. After he served everyone, he reached into his jacket pocket to retrieve a pack of cigarettes and a lighter. He tapped the bottom of the pack to extend the tops of several cigarettes. "Would you care for one, Mrs. Lewis?" Jessie graciously accepted his offer of a light. "Mr. Lewis?" Empy took one too.

They both watched to see what would happen next. He did

indeed offer one to Helen who accepted it without a word. She had never smoked or had a drink in the house before, but clearly this was a ritual with which she and Dick were quite familiar.

Jessie locked eyes with Empy as she said, "An excellent Old Fashioned, wouldn't you say?"

Empy nodded, and she continued, "Helen tells us that you're from Colorado. None of us has been west of the Mississippi. What's it like?"

Conversation flowed easily. At some point they moved to the table, where the conversation continued. They learned that Dick had two brothers, one in the postal section of the Navy expecting to be deployed to Hawaii. His second brother was in airport administration in Wichita. He, his mother, and his brothers had moved from Connecticut to Colorado in search of his father, who had gone west to find work in the middle of the Depression, but had never returned. They found him in Colorado with another woman. Dick's parents divorced, but his mother had happily remarried.

Although he didn't say so, Jessie realized that Dick had grown up quite poor. He kept expressing his gratitude to his high school chemistry teacher for walking him across the street to the Chemistry Department at Colorado College and convincing the chairman that Dick should be admitted on scholarship. Despite her resolve to reserve judgment at this first meeting, she realized that she liked him. Once more she and Empy exchanged glances, and Empy nodded ever so slightly. Jessie gave in to her impulse.

"You must join us for a weekend in Bethany Beach as soon as it is warm enough. You can stay at the inn just up the street from our friends' cottage. Have you ever seen the ocean?"

"Oh, I would enjoy that! I've been once with some of my buddies, and I was just getting the hang of body surfing when we had to leave."

"Thank you, Mother. That's a generous invitation."

Ada entered to clear the dessert dishes. Dick grinned at her.

"Popovers, eh? I've never seen a better container for gobs and gobs of butter! So delicious! And the roast beef was pretty good too!"

"Oh, Dr. Brooks. I bet butter melts in your mouth even better than in popovers!" she laughed, clearly pleased.

"What new delicacy will you make next time?"

"Maybe buckwheat cakes and scrapple, but you'd have to come for breakfast."

Everyone smiled.

Dick rose. "This has been a wonderful evening. I shouldn't overstay my welcome. Thank you, Helen." He approached her chair, and for a horrifying second, Jessie thought he would kiss her. Thankfully he just pulled her chair back as she rose.

"I'll see him out." Helen and Dick left the dining room together.

1.13

Mrs. Richard Ensign Brooks

Jessie stood in front of the mirror in their bedroom. For a moment, Sophronia stared back at her, but the image faded to reveal the mother of the bride. Their corsages were similar, but Sophronia had worn a gauzy dress of chiffon while the mother of the bride wore a tailored suit. Sophronia's face had carried the hopefulness of youth while the face of the mother of the bride bore the emerging lines of middle age. Ada had assisted Sophronia; this time Ada was assisting the bride.

Down the hall, Ada was pinning a corsage on the lapel of Helen's suit. Made of cream-colored brocade, it reminded Jessie of her sister Helen's wedding to Caleb ten years before. Jessie had believed her sister would have a second chance at happiness when she had remarried in 1931, but Caleb had died even sooner than Eric. Neither marriage had reached its first anniversary.

Helen and Dick had decided on a small wedding. For one thing, only Dick's brother, Howard, who would be his best man, would represent his family. Travel from Texas for his father, Wyoming for his mother, and Kansas for his younger brother was much too expensive. For another thing, with the Germans occupying Paris, the desperate escape at Dunkirk, the blitz on London, the relentless submarine attacks on shipping, and the bellicose behavior of Japan, this did not seem to be the moment for any extravagance. Jessie and Empy both approved the couple's decision to put their savings into a house. A brick house in a brand new suburban development, Edgemoor Terrace, with three bedrooms, two bathrooms, and an attached garage for Dick's Buick, seemed like such an excellent investment. In fact, Jessie felt a twinge of envy. She and Empy had never bought a house. Instead they had invested their money in the pharmacy.

Jessie noticed that the church was pleasantly full. She was pleased that her closest friends were there—Lura Wood, who had introduced them to Bethany Beach, and Ruth Cann, who had sponsored her membership in the Washington Heights Century Club. She nodded to Helen's friends from high school—including Elva and Louise, who had also appeared in the Coca-Cola advertisement. Her sisters, Eva, Mary, and Helen, had traveled with Mother from Philadelphia. And she was proud to see some strange faces she knew must be colleagues from the DuPont Company. Helen was marrying up.

Dick and his brother Howard both looked endearingly nervous as Empy walked Helen up the aisle. Despite her gloomy mood before she had left home, Jessie smiled. After the ceremony, the gaiety of the reception in the church social hall was infectious, and she relaxed in anticipation of the small, elegant dinner that would follow for family and out of town guests at the University Club.

Just then, Howard clinked a glass.

"May I have your attention! I want to propose a toast to my big brother, who has driven me crazy for years! Do you believe that when he left for Ohio State, he left me a desk on the top of which he had carved the command "Study, damn you, study!"

Everyone chuckled.

"Well, I spent many years trying to escape his commands, but what a good thing that he took his own advice. Here he is working for the DuPont Company, where he found the prettiest girl east of the Mississippi! Congratulations and years of happiness to Dr. and Mrs. Richard E. Brooks!"

"Here, here!" came back in a cheer.

About 10 o'clock, Helen and Dick pulled away from the University Club showered in confetti, with streamers flying and cans clattering behind them. They were headed for the Hotel DuPont for their wedding night and then to Boston for a short honeymoon. For both of them, the pressures at work were intense; they could not afford to be away long. As if they had been prescient, one week after their return, the Japanese would bomb Pearl Harbor. Had they waited to be married, there would have been no honeymoon at all.

Yes, Jessie thought, *there goes Mrs. Richard E. Brooks.* She saw that Empy waved with his face frozen into a forced smile; she would barely notice Helen's absence, but Empy and Ada would miss her acutely.

1.14

Clouds Gathering

Helen and Dick dove back into their jobs. The shock of the attack on Pearl Harbor deepened their commitment to their work. Jessie and Empy settled into a pattern of alternating Sunday dinners, first at their house where Ada cooked and was delighted to have an opportunity to see Helen, and then at the home of the newlyweds, where Helen was doing a passable job of learning to cook—thanks to Ada's Sunday coaching.

At one of these dinners, Helen brought up an entirely new topic.

"Do you remember the article in *The Saturday Evening Post* about the new organization called Alcoholics Anonymous? It appeared last spring sometime."

Jessie did remember it. She always read T*he Saturday Evening Post* from cover to cover, usually the day it arrived. At the time this issue had appeared, she had been pleased because it spoke directly to a local problem. Wilmington had a large population of Irish and Italian immigrants, whom everyone knew were heavy drinkers who caused a great deal of trouble. Alcoholics Anonymous seemed like an organization that might help restore public decorum.

"I do," Jessie replied. "Why are you mentioning it?"

"Well, the DuPont Company has begun hiring recovering alcoholics to run AA groups within the company. Several were hired this week. We all know about the labor shortage as so many men go into the military, so it's important that every possible person is available to work. I applaud the Company for establishing this policy."

Dick chimed in. "Yes, we need laboratory assistants, people to care for the laboratory animals, cleaners—we have every sort of job you can think of. My colleagues and I are proud of the Company for implementing the very newest ideas."

"Why would you hire recovering men? Wouldn't you want them to be fully recovered?" Jessie asked.

"That's exactly the point—they will be recovering for the rest of their lives. One of the core principles of AA is lifelong abstinence," Helen answered.

Jessie laughed as she picked up her glass and clinked the ice cubes. "Well, I'm glad that principle doesn't apply to us! Don't you agree, Empy?"

Empy smiled weakly. "Right," he said.

By the summer of 1942, Jessie had to admit it—she was bored. Although she had jumped enthusiastically into the war efforts of the new Century Club, she missed the bridge tournaments and theatrical presentations that were now on hold. And, more than she had expected, she missed Helen. She had not realized how much she had looked forward to Helen's stories from work and the excitement of the bustle of Helen's friends coming in and out. There was no life left in the house. Empy left for the pharmacy before she got up. In the evening, without Helen, they couldn't seem to keep a conversation going at the dinner table, and by the time she entered the living room after cleaning up, Empy was invariably dozing in his chair. She had started going straight upstairs to read until she was drowsy enough to turn out the light. She never heard Empy come to bed.

As a solution to her boredom, she had been mulling over a letter to her sister Mary to inquire about returning to work at her employment agency. One stifling August afternoon, she wrote the letter and walked to the corner to mail it. Mary responded immediately and enthusiastically. *I'm overwhelmed with requests for all sorts of workers,* she wrote. *Maybe you can help me figure out how to encourage more women to apply. The demand is unbelievable!*

The very next Monday, Jessie caught the 7:10 a.m. train to Philadelphia for her first day on the job. Now she was out of the house before Empy was, and they fell into a pattern of getting their own meals during the week. She was too tired to cook when she arrived home about 6:30 p.m. Empy completely understood.

Jessie loved the bustle in Mary's office. The phone rang constantly; people walked in off the street; she was in charge of a huge project. From the first moment Mary had asked for ideas about recruiting women, Jessie had been thinking hard about the problem. In the very first week, she made Mary a proposal.

"What if I make an appointment at the personnel office of the Philadelphia Navy Yard to explore the jobs open to women? Then we design a series of posters that appeal to women's yearning to support the boys in the war. We could offer to do initial screening for the Yard and then send them candidates with knowledge of what is expected and confidence that they can learn the jobs. We could distribute the posters throughout the city."

Jessie explained her proposal in one breath. Finally she inhaled. "What do you think?" she concluded.

Mary hesitated. This was not like anything her employment agency had done before. There would be many details—developing a basic understanding of the jobs, how her agency would be compensated, and, not to be underestimated, the difficulty of working with a male organization. But Jessie's enthusiasm was infectious. And Mary knew her sister would be bold because Jessie loved being on stage.

"Let's give it a try," she said.

"I'm going to call right this minute," Jessie said as she jumped out of her chair. Mary was not at all surprised that Jessie had the phone number for the Navy Yard personnel office at her fingertips.

The personnel official loved the idea. "We would hire dogs if we thought we could teach them to hold a welding torch," the man said. "Some of the boys won't like women in their space," he continued, "but they will hold their tongues—for the most part. Tell your gals they will need thick skin, but if it gets too bad, we'll deal with it."

Ah, yes, Jessie thought, *this is a topic we'll have to include in our screenings.* "Okay," she said.

On the way out the door, she had a fleeting thought. *They would hire dogs if they could weld, the man had said. What about Negroes? What about boys like Floyd*? But that was too big a thought to wrap her mind around; she dismissed it.

Back at home, Jessie noticed Empy had grown even more

quiet. Occasionally she inquired about the pharmacy. "It's going fine. Yes, we do see shortages of some medicines and other items we would normally stock, but it's okay." He would then ask her about the employment agency, and she loved the opportunity to describe the booming success of the partnership with the Navy Yard. Empy would nod, but he never seemed to share the excitement she felt for her work.

By the spring of 1944, everyone could feel the momentum shifting. Everywhere, talk was about an impending invasion of Europe. Although the fighting was brutal, the Allies seemed to be moving relentlessly north from island to island in the Pacific. Evidently Helen and Dick also felt optimistic too because one Sunday, they had an announcement.

Dick clinked his glass; Jessie stopped mid-sentence. "You're going to be grandparents!" he said with a grin. Helen smiled awkwardly.

"Well, I was beginning to wonder," Jessie said. "This is very good news."

"Congratulations!" Empy concurred.

He and Helen locked eyes and exchanged imperceptible smiles.

"When?" Jessie asked.

"Early in the new year," Dick replied. "We believe the war will be winding down by then, and Helen can stop working in good conscience. We want several children, and we're not getting any younger. We have waited long enough."

"Well, I was 25 when I had Helen. She will only be 27 then, but I do see what you mean if you want to have several children. Empy and I lost our second ...," her voice trailed off, and she avoided Empy's eyes.

"We'll have to plan a baby shower. That will be such fun! I haven't hosted a real party since the war started!" Jessie continued.

As the parents-to-be took their leave, Empy shook Dick's hand vigorously and hugged his daughter tenderly.

Helen whispered in his ear. "Let's meet for dinner soon. I feel like we haven't had a good talk in ages."

"I would love that," Empy whispered back.

Helen and Empy met at the Columbus Inn about a week later.

"How are you, Empy—really?"

Empy changed the subject. "The important question is how are you?" he asked.

"I'm just fine. The doctor says everything is progressing normally. He doesn't want me to gain too much weight, and he would prefer that I stop smoking. But smoking helps dull my appetite so stopping is not something I plan on doing," she replied with a smile. "So there's not much to talk about with me. How are *you*?" she repeated.

Empy was quiet. Even though it had been almost three years since she had married and left the house, she and Empy still maintained their special connection. Helen knew he had something to say; she would wait.

He went on to tell her that nothing was the same since she left, and that Jessie was full of her own life—as always. "I don't think she really knows I exist. And actually, I don't care," he said dispiritedly.

He went on to explain how the pharmacy used to be his sanctuary, particularly once she and her friends began to congregate there. "You brought such life and energy to the store—and to me. Now I am bored. You are not there, and so many other regulars aren't either. The war has upset everyone's routines. I've been opening later and closing earlier. No one seems to notice."

Helen felt a chill. She had noticed her father's withdrawal, but had pushed it out of her consciousness. *Not only is Jessie full of her own life, but I am too,* she thought. *It is such a relief to have escaped from Mother, and to have been freed from my continuous disappointment in her detachment. But Empy has been left behind in that sterile household, and he is suffering.*

"Please don't think I'm not happy about your work, Dick, and the baby. I want nothing but the best for you, and I am thrilled that you have it. It just leaves a hole, that's all," he continued so softly that Helen had to strain to hear him.

A hole, Helen thought with a flash of anger, *that should be filled by life with your loving wife.*

"Empy, I understand and I'm so sorry," she said. "Would it help if we saw each other more frequently? At least until the baby comes, we could meet for dinner every week."

They both knew this was a stopgap measure, but she could think of nothing else.

"I would like that," he said.

To the waitress he said, "I'll have another Manhattan, please."

1.15

Babies

Jessie was pleased when Dick called to tell her that the new baby had arrived safely, that she was a girl, and that they were naming her Helen Lewis Brooks. This baby would be the fourth Helen, following Mother Helen, sister Helen, and daughter Helen. Really, she thought, what other name was appropriate—unless maybe they named the baby for her grandmother?

Out loud she said, "Little Helen! How wonderful! Congratulations! How is Big Helen?"

"She is still quite groggy, but with the total anesthesia they use these days, she didn't suffer one bit. She and Little Helen will still be in the hospital for five more days. I will let you know when you can visit," Dick replied.

And so it was established. The Helens would be distinguished by the prefixes Big and Little.

"Yes, by all means. Empy will be so pleased to hear this news. He has been worried as the time has gotten closer. Helen—Big Helen, that is—is the apple of his eye, you know." And she hastened to add, "Little Helen will be too, I'm sure."

Jessie felt Dick's smile through the phone. "I'm sure that's true," he said. "Empy is the kindest, gentlest, warmest person I know. I'll call again in a day or two. Maybe you both can talk to Big Helen then."

Jessie's thoughts turned to Empy, who was sitting in his chair on this Saturday afternoon, working a crossword puzzle. Maybe the news of the birth would cheer him up. On the other hand, now that the baby was here, his weekly dinners with Helen would end. Jessie knew they had been the highlight of his week. Other than that one day each week when his step lightened, he was morose, almost sullen. She was beginning to wonder what was bothering him.

"Empy," she called excitedly. "That was Dick. Helen has had a little girl, another Helen. They are both fine, and we can visit in a few days. Isn't that terrific news?"

Empy lifted his head, and she noticed his eyes were slightly bloodshot.

"Yes," he replied flatly, "I'm very glad." He returned to his crossword puzzle without asking for any details. Ignoring Empy's tone, Jessie returned to the kitchen, where she was preparing dinner.

As soon as Helen regained her strength, she, Dick, and her parents resumed their Sunday dinners, now always at Jessie's. Ada combined cooking with babysitting, taking full responsibility for Little Helen as soon as her parents brought her through the door.

Each Sunday presented an opportunity to discuss the latest news of the war, which now came fast and furiously.

On a brilliant spring day, Jessie proclaimed a toast. "Here's to victory in Europe!! If I hadn't been at work in Philadelphia, I wouldn't have missed the joyous, raucous celebration in Caesar Rodney Square! Empy could hear it from the pharmacy as he watched people stream by, right Empy?"

"Yes," he agreed. "I doubt there has been that much excitement in the center of Wilmington since Caesar Rodney himself returned to declare that, on behalf of Delaware, he had cast the decisive vote in favor of the Declaration of Independence!"

"We still have the war in the Pacific to worry about," Dick cautioned.

The other three nodded, acutely aware that Howard was stationed in some unknown place in the Pacific.

A few months later, they tried to digest the terrifying news of the bombings of Hiroshima and Nagasaki.

"This enormous destructive force results from nuclear fission," Dick explained.

"All those innocent civilians killed," Helen interrupted. "What if the Japanese had dropped a bomb like that on Pearl Harbor? Everyone would have been dead; the war would have been lost before we could regroup."

"But," Jessie asserted, "we developed it first—before the Japanese or the Germans. This action will save the lives of thousands of boys who otherwise would die fighting island to island until they reached Tokyo."

Once again, everyone's thoughts turned to Howard. The celebratory mood of the crowd in Rodney Square following the news of Japan's unconditional surrender exceeded the exuberance of the earlier celebration —if that were possible. At the next Sunday dinner, even Helen celebrated without restraint.

By the summer of 1946, shortages of consumer goods were rapidly disappearing. Only sugar was still being rationed. The nature of the work at Mary's employment business had shifted as soldiers returned and were discharged to seek work in burgeoning factories and offices. Jessie continued her daily travel to Philadelphia; Empy reported that business at the pharmacy had improved; Dick said that research in his lab was leading to the successful adaptation of many war-time compounds used in the war to consumer goods. Nylon made excellent ladies' stockings, he noted one Sunday with a smile.

At a family gathering that fall attended by all four generations— Great-grandmother Helen; sisters Jessie, Helen, Mary, and Eva; Big Helen; Little Helen—Dick announced the expected arrival of their second child the following spring.

"We already have a female junior so, without a doubt, this one will be Richard Ensign Brooks, Jr.," he pronounced with conviction. He could not quite conceal his disappointment when he called Jessie months later to say that a second girl had arrived—this one named for his mother, Marion Smith Brooks.

"The baby is quite small," he said, "barely five pounds. Helen is fine, but they will keep the baby in the hospital a bit longer."

◆ ◆ ◆

Throughout the war, Ada had continued to work for Jessie and Empy. She cleaned, ironed, and made dinner for them on Sundays and on the other days when she was there. One day a few months before Marion was born, Helen approached Jessie.

"Mother," she began. "With a second baby coming, I could use some help. I wonder if you would share Ada—maybe two

Left to right standing: The first Helen, Jessie's mother; Eva and Mary, Jessie's sisters; the third Helen, Jessie's daughter; the second Helen, Jessie's sister

Kneeling: Jessie and the fourth Helen, Jessie's granddaughter

days at your house ... and two days at mine?"

Empy answered immediately. "Of course. We can get along just fine with Ada here two days each week. Can't we, Jessie?" he concluded, looking at Jessie directly.

Jessie fumed. The two of them were still in cahoots. She wanted to protest loudly, "No, I cannot!" But something made her bite her tongue. Empy spoke up so rarely about anything; it was good to see him perk up.

"Okay," she said. "I'll talk it over with Ada."

Ada melded seamlessly into the Brooks household. She became the repository of stories that made everybody laugh. Stories about the babies were particular favorites, especially the one about Marion, who she claimed was a baby with "quar actions," which she would demonstrate lovingly with wild gesticulations accompanied by gales of laughter.

Jessie had to agree when, after a holiday dinner which Ada cooked, Empy said, "Aren't you glad you agreed to share Ada? How else would we have all ended up in stitches in the kitchen?"

In 1949, to her great delight, Jessie enjoyed the fulfillment of two longtime wishes: a namesake and a cottage in Bethany Beach. The third girl, Jessie Townsend Brooks, arrived in March. In June, the family of five, plus a nurse for infant Jessie, headed to Bethany for the first of many summers at the cottage one block away from the Atlantic Ocean. Jessie's longtime friend, Lura Wood, who owned a cottage across the sandy street, had alerted Helen and Dick to the For Sale sign in the front yard of the shingled corner house. With an enclosed front porch, living room, dining area, small kitchen, bedroom, and bathroom on the first floor, and two bedrooms tucked under the steeply sloping roof on the second floor, it was perfect.

"On weekends you and Empy can stay with us," Lura told Jessie excitedly. "We can easily find another couple and have two tables for bridge, just like we used to do when Dick was courting Helen," she added. "It will be great fun!"

With a warm glow in her voice, Jessie replied, "Maybe the war is really over at last, and we can all get back to normal." *Perhaps even Empy,* she hoped.

After a pause following three babies, each two years apart, girl #4 arrived in 1952. Named Mary Amelia after Jessie's sister, from birth she was called Amy to avoid possible confu-

Clockwise: Cousin Jane Townsend, Empy, Dick holding Amy, Woo, Helen #2, Aunt Helena, neighbor, Eva, and Mary and Helen who were Jessie's sisters.

Children clockwise: Helen, Jessie, Marion.

sion with her sister Marion. Jessie and Empy may have visited Helen and Amy in the hospital as they had when their three other granddaughters were born, but they would never develop as close a relationship with Amy as they had with Helen, Marion, and Jessie. Before Amy could walk, Jessie and Empy had fled from Wilmington.

Part 2

Woo and Me

(1945-1987)

2.1

The Silver Flask

I leaned on the windowsill, watching eagerly for the green Plymouth to roll into the driveway.

"They're here! Papoo and Woowoo are here!" I announced excitedly. My sisters joined me at the front door. The three of us loved visits from our grandparents. This time, they would be staying past our bedtimes because Mother and Daddy were going out, which made this visit special indeed.

"I have hot dogs and baked beans warming for their supper, and a bottle for Jessie at bedtime," Mother instructed as she put on her coat. "Remember to cut Jessie's hot dogs into very small pieces. Dick and I will be home around 10. Put Jessie down at 7, but Helen and Marion can stay up until 7:30."

I was thrilled. I knew I could count on staying up even longer.

Once Jessie was settled with her bottle after we had our dinner, Woo returned to the living room to ask, "Would you like me to play the piano?"

"Oh, yes!" both Marion and I cried. "We'll dance!" So we did—whirling around the room as Papoo beamed at our antics, until we were too out of breath to twirl one more time.

"Okay, time for bed ... and stories! Upstairs you go."

"The pirates!" I cried, "... tell us the stories about the pirates ... and when you went shooting bullfrogs with Floyd!"

"Yes, yes," Woo replied, "... once you're in your nightgowns with both hair and teeth brushed. But don't wake Jessie when you go up."

Once we were tucked in our beds, Woo settled in a chair beside us. "Once upon a time," she began, "... there was a little girl who lived by a river. One day as she and her friend Floyd paddled by the former hideout of the bandit Patty Cannon, they heard voices ...,"

We were transported ... right to sleep.

After Sunday dinner at our house, Papoo loved to take me for a drive in his beloved green Plymouth. Often we went to the Wilmington Zoo where I loved watching the monkeys. Or sometimes to Rockland Park where I had recently learned to pump my legs on the swings.

As we set out one day, I startled Papoo by demanding, "I want to sip from the silver flask too!" I didn't think it was fair that he got a special drink on our trips, but I did not.

Papoo was bent over in the driver's seat with his hand on the silver flask stashed beneath it. He began every drive with a swig or two, and it evidently had never occurred to him that I was watching him intently.

"It's not fair," I insisted. "Everybody tells me to share, but you aren't sharing!"

He hastily shoved the flask back under the seat. "That's for grownups only—not children."

"Well, I still don't think it's fair," I replied sulkily as I wedged myself against the passenger door.

Papoo backed out of the driveway and headed to the park. Neither of us spoke. I could tell that the frosty atmosphere in the car was making Empy sad, but to fix it, all he had to do was share! What had been a magical event each Sunday had suddenly become a disappointment for both of us. I just couldn't understand why he was being so stubborn.

When we arrived at the park, Papoo opened the passenger door and said gruffly, "Go play on the swings now. I'll watch you from here."

"I think you're a meanie!" I said, sliding off the seat. I stomped away. Papoo returned to the driver's seat and pulled out the silver flask.

Without Papoo pushing me or sitting on a nearby bench cheering me on, swinging was not much fun. I headed back to the car where I had to bang on the window to get his attention.

"I want to go home now," I demanded.

"Okay," he said as he struggled to open his door. He held the car as he moved to the passenger side, opening the door so I could climb in. Back in the driver's seat, he put the car in reverse and swung the steering wheel to move out of the parking spot. Somehow the front fender hit the car on his right.

I shrieked as I was jostled, "Papoo, you hit that car!"

"It's nothing," he responded as he backed out a second time and steered resolutely for the park exit.

When we got home, Papoo did not get out of the car to come around and open my door. The next thing that happened? Mother was knocking on the glass of Papoo's car window.

"Empy!" she cried. "Are you all right? The car is cockeyed. What happened?"

"Helen," Dick said from the opposite side where he had extracted me from the car. "The right fender is damaged and the headlight is broken."

"Daddy, Papoo hit the car next to us when we were leaving the park. He drove funny all the way home. I was scared!"

Daddy looked at me in disbelief when I said, "And I was mad at him. He wouldn't let me drink from his silver flask. We didn't have any fun at all!"

Mother and Daddy locked eyes. "What flask?" Daddy asked.

"Under his seat," I told him. "He drinks from it all the time, but he won't share!"

Daddy said to Mommy, "I'm going to take Little Helen into the house. You stay here with your father. We'll see if we can't get him into the house when I get back; then I'll retrieve this flask."

Jessie had been standing on the front lawn watching and listening. The small pit which had been residing in her stomach for some time had exploded. She thought she might be sick.

Helen and Dick managed to get Empy into the house.

"Empy," Helen pleaded as she knelt in front of him cradling his hand, "What happened? Little Helen says you hit another car? Why did you park the car on the grass instead of in the driveway?"

Empy didn't remember. "I don't know." He was leaning forward, mumbling— his head hanging.

Dick entered the room with the silver flask. "Sniff this," he said to Helen and Jessie.

Helen shook her head. "I can smell his breath. I know what the flask smells like."

Jessie reluctantly took a whiff and instantly recoiled.

Helen snapped. "Mother, you have to face reality! Empy is a drunk. You've been in denial for years, and we almost had a tragedy! We have to deal with this now. He can hardly hold himself up in the chair!"

Dick intervened. "I think we should take him to the emergency room now. I know from working with the Personnel Department at DuPont that they will evaluate him there and make recommendations. Jessie, you must come with me. Helen will stay here with the children."

Abruptly, Jessie and Helen became aware of me cowering on the stairs with my sisters. "Daddy," I whispered, "... will Papoo be all right?"

"Yes, Toodie," he answered, using his pet nickname for me as he picked me up gently. "We will take Papoo to the hospital where they can make him better."

Jessie was in shock, humiliated. For the first time in her life, she was unable to function. Once again, her sisters took charge. First they arranged a twenty-eight day stay at the Philadelphia Detox Center. Next, after Jessie had spent a week hibernating at home, Mary called.

"Jessie," Mary insisted, "you simply must return to work. If for no other reason, you need the income. The store is closed, and who knows what will happen with it. Even more importantly, you have to get out of the house. You can't hide forever!"

"I can't face anyone," Jessie said, "even Helen. She is so angry at me."

"Come to work. People here don't know what happened. You can spend a couple nights with us, and we can help you make plans. And you have to visit Empy and talk to the counselors."

"Okay," she replied weakly. "Thank you."

At the dinner table the first night of her stay in her sisters' apartment, Jessie was almost mute. Helen tried hard to draw her out.

"Jessie," she said in a gentle, but concerned voice, "... imagine yourself a year from now. Where will you and Empy be? What will you be doing?"

"I don't know," Jessie replied. "I just know that I can never show my face in Wilmington society again."

"Well then, let's figure out someplace else where you can live," Helen replied matter of factly. "Let's see if there's anything back in Snow Hill or somewhere nearby."

The next day, Jessie visited Empy for the first time. She dreaded seeing him. Her feelings were in such a jumble of anger, guilt, and fear. What should she say?

Empy was waiting at a corner table in the large sunny common room. Geraniums bloomed in the window. Two other people played cards at a table across the room. What looked like a family was gathered in a cluster of easy chairs in another corner. The setting was comforting, and Jessie relaxed a bit. She sat down across from Empy. He spoke first.

"I am so very sorry," he began. "I know I endangered Little Helen and, for that, I will never forgive myself."

And what about me, she thought. *You have destroyed my life.*

"And I know I have embarrassed you terribly," Empy continued. "Can you forgive me?"

She waited for him to go on, but he did not. As the silence grew, she realized it was her turn to speak. She wanted to scream and spew out every hurt. She surprised herself when she did not.

"Yes," she said evenly. "You did endanger Little Helen, and you have humiliated me. I don't know if I can forgive you, not now anyway, but we have to decide what we are going to do. I can't live in Wilmington any longer."

"I understand," he said. "I hope you can forgive me in time, and that— eventually—we can discuss how we got to this place."

She bristled. *Was he going to blame her ...?!*

He noticed her tense up. "Don't worry. We are both too raw to have that conversation now. The counselors are encouraging me to make concrete plans that include ongoing attendance at Alcoholics Anonymous meetings and postponing discussion of our deep issues for now. And I think I could benefit from a change of scenery myself."

Okay, she thought. *That's exactly what my sisters are working on.*

The sign on the pharmacy door said *Closed Due to Illness.* It stayed there for weeks. Upon reopening, customers were astonished to be greeted by an ebullient young man who explained to each of the regulars:

"Mr. Lewis has decided to retire for health reasons. I am your new pharmacist, and I promise I will serve you with the same care he provided. He has left meticulous records."

Then he personalized his message. "You are Mrs. Smith? Yes, I see here that you were due a refill two weeks ago. Let me provide that plus thirty extra tablets to compensate for the delay."

And when Mrs. Smith expressed her deep regret about

Mr. Lewis's health issues and asked that her concern be passed on, the young pharmacist replied, "Of course. Mr. Lewis will be so pleased to hear from you." But in fact, the young pharmacist had never met Mr. Lewis, and none of these messages of concern would ever reach him. The young pharmacist had bought the business through an agent at a very good price. With the help of Jessie's sisters, the pharmacy had been sold, Empy had a new job with Delaware Ice and Coal as a sales representative in Sussex County, and they had rented a charming old house in Lewes. It would be a fresh start.

Several months later, early in the morning on a brisk spring day, I was once again leaning on the windowsill, waiting for the green Plymouth to pull into the driveway. Rather than being filled with excitement as usual, this time I was full of dread and confusion. I had not seen Papoo or Woowoo for a very long time. Mommy said that Papoo was in a hospital getting better, and Woo was busy visiting him there.

"Why can't we visit too?" I kept asking.

"It's not a place for children," Mother said repeatedly. "You will see them again when he is released."

"When will that be?" I persisted.

"I don't know!" Mother said with exasperation. "I'll tell you when I do, so stop pestering me!" I slunk away.

Woowoo and Papoo drove the repaired and fully loaded Plymouth into the driveway. I knew that they were here to say goodbye because they were moving to a rented house in Lewes, Delaware. I couldn't wait to give each of them the biggest hug.

"The Lewises are moving to Lewes!" Papoo called gaily as

he waved through the open window. "We'll see you in the summer when you come to Bethany." Woo smiled bravely and waved too.

"Aren't they coming in?" I cried, astonished. "We haven't seen them in so long!"

"Oh, no," Mother replied, "... it's a long drive to their new home in Lewes, but don't worry. That's very near Bethany, so we will see them frequently during the summer."

By now, I knew not to protest. I knew not to ask if the silver flask was under the front seat because somehow it was part of this upheaval in our lives. Had I been wrong to tell Daddy about it? My heart sank; I turned away feeling abandoned and lost.

22

King's Highway, Lewes

Jessie was standing in the kitchen of the rented house on King's Highway, surveying the stack of moving boxes, when she heard a knock on the door. She opened it, and a woman breezed in with a basket over her arm and a pot in her hand. She rushed by Jessie to put the pot on the counter.

"That's heavy," she said. "I was sure I was going to drop it before you answered the door. It's a beef stew, and here in this basket are biscuits to go with it." Surveying the boxes herself, she continued, "I knew you would have too much to do to cook!"

Jessie was flabbergasted; she had never seen this woman before in her life.

"I'm Mary Reed, your next-door neighbor. I've been waiting impatiently for you to arrive. This house has been empty since Mr. Simpson died, and there hasn't been a woman here since his wife died two years before that. I just know we are going to be great friends! Now shall we get to work unpacking these boxes?"

Jessie opened her mouth to shout *Get out! How dare you barge into my house, my privacy, my life!* Mary's stream of chatter continued before she could get a word out.

"I know your name is Jessie Lewis, and that your husband

is Milton, and that he travels for Delaware Ice and Coal, and that your daughter and granddaughters live in Wilmington. That makes you almost as alone as I am. I'm a widow, six years now, and we were never blessed with children. You and I will have each other! How about if I open boxes, unwrap things, and hand them to you to put away? One woman can never set up another woman's kitchen."

Mary picked up the scissors on the kitchen table and snipped the string on a box in front of her.

"Ah, this box has dishes. Maybe they should go in that cupboard?" She handed Jessie a dinner plate, pointing to a cupboard near the stove.

As if hypnotized, Jessie took the dinner plate and put it in the cupboard. Soon the cupboard held twelve dinner plates, salad plates, bread and butter plates, bowls, and cups and saucers.

"There," Mary said. "Perfect!"

The rhythmic motion of receiving dishes from Mary, placing them in the cupboard, then turning to receive the next was calming. Jessie found her voice.

"How do you know so much about me?" she asked tentatively.

"Oh, Angela told me. She's the real estate agent, and she goes to the Presbyterian Church with me, and she's in our craft group and our bridge club. Do you play bridge?"

Bridge. Jessie's flood of memories of bridge tournaments at the Century Club provoked a visceral reaction. Her stomach clenched; her throat went dry; her upper lip broke out in drops of sweat. Seemingly Mary didn't notice.

"We meet tomorrow night, two tables at Mabel's house.

If we have more than eight, we rotate people in and out. You can just walk across your driveway to mine and jump in my car—7:20 p.m. should work. And we can do the same thing for church on Sunday, at 10:45 a.m. I like to get there early. If Milton is home by then, he should come too. I'm sure you don't want to go by yourselves."

"Okay," Jessie found herself saying. "And he goes by Empy."

"Empy?" Mary inquired. "That's unusual."

"It's his initials—M.P. How did you know he's not home?"

"No car in the driveway. If he weren't on the road, he and the car would both be here," Mary smiled.

"Oh," Jessie replied. Hunkering down alone in her house was not going to be possible here. She took a deep breath.

"We've unpacked cups and saucers. How about some tea? And maybe one of your biscuits? I have some jam in the ice box."

"Wonderful." Mary grinned.

Jessie and Empy settled into a rhythm of their own. With Mary's support and encouragement, they became members of the Lewes Presbyterian Church where Empy was elected a deacon. He joined the Lion's Club, which asked him to be their representative on the committee to judge Christmas decorations. He was especially pleased by their choice in the Negro division, with fond memories of Ada reverberating as the committee drove through the Negro neighborhood. A few months later, he was elected Lions Club secretary.

Jessie's bridge game sharpened to the point where she was in high demand as a partner in duplicate tournaments. She joined Mary's craft group and was quite proud of the red felt Christmas tree skirt she adorned with sequins. Even though it didn't approach the quality of the samplers that her sisters had stitched back in Snow Hill days, she thought it was good enough to give Helen.

Empy traveled Monday through Thursday—sometimes gone for day trips; other times, overnights. She made a point of preparing a nice dinner on Thursday evenings. It did not include cocktails. The gloomy silences of dinners in the last year of their lives in Wilmington were replaced with chitchat about their daily lives and discussion of news from Wilmington which arrived in Helen's letters. Little Helen had started kindergarten at the Tatnall School. They had bought a second car for Dick's commute so Helen could leave the house with the three younger girls in tow. Jessie and Empy did not discuss the circumstances of their move with each other or in letters to their daughter.

Just as Mother had promised, we saw Papoo and Woowoo regularly during our summer stays in the cottage at Bethany. Papoo and Woowoo would drive the twenty miles from Lewes to Bethany Beach several times during the six weeks that my mother, my sisters, and I spent at the cottage, with Daddy coming on weekends and on his two-week vacation. At the end of that time, on the way back to Wilmington, Mother and Daddy would deposit me in Lewes for my annual stay. I got to know Mary, Papoo and Woo's neighbor and Woo's very good friend, and the boy across the street with whom I had my first flirtation. Summer at Bethany had always been special, and now that special time extended to include my stays with Woo and Papoo in Lewes.

23

Papoo and Me

One Thursday evening at the dinner table, Empy startled Jessie by announcing, "I have had a letter from Arthur Morris asking me to consider managing his Rexall Drug Store downtown. I'm to meet him there tomorrow."

Jessie looked up. "Arthur Morris? The man you knew through the Pharmacy Association?"

"Yes, exactly. I'm interested. After all, a pharmacist is what I am, and I would love to be off the road. I think Mary encouraged him to contact me."

A jumble of thoughts flashed through Jessie's mind. Art Morris must know about The Great Humiliation, memories of which no longer tormented her every day. She had built a good life—not on the social level of her Wilmington life, but this wasn't Wilmington. She was safe now. Would all this be jeopardized if Empy went back to his old world?

"We have a nice life now," she began. Empy recoiled.

Although he didn't complain, selling ice and coal on the road could not be satisfying, Jessie acknowledged to herself. Furthermore, being the wife of the pharmacist at the main drug store in town felt like a step up for her too. She regrouped.

"But I understand that you would like to be back in a drug

store. After all, you worked hard to earn your license. I hope the meeting goes well."

The meeting went very well, and by the next summer, Papoo was in charge at the Rexall Drug Store on Second Street. I loved Papoo's drug store. Although Papoo told me many times it was not his drug store—he was managing it for his friend, Authur Morris—I ignored that irrelevant fact. From my perspective, it was his. If it wasn't, then how come I received all those special privileges during my visits there? I got to enter through the rear door while ordinary people had to enter through the front. I got to walk into Papoo's private work space lined with tall shelves filled with all sorts of bottles and jars. I loved the smells—musky and medicinal and magical. I loved watching Papoo reach for a particular bottle, count out a certain number of pills into a small vial, type a label with two fingers, and then stick it on the vial. I loved following him through the swinging doors into the public space where he would present the vial to the customer, receive money, then press buttons on the cash register to make the drawer pop open. I flushed with pleasure when he introduced me to the customer as his granddaughter and special assistant, or, even better, when a customer recognized me and said hello. I loved hopping up on a stool at the soda fountain and slurping a Cherry Coke made just for me by the soda jerk.

At first, I didn't like the beach at Lewes as much as the beach at Bethany; it was on the Delaware Bay, which didn't have the waves of the Atlantic Ocean. But Woo had introduced me to children who lived right near the beach, and playing with them was so much fun that I didn't miss the

Papoo in Lewes

waves much at all. A few years later, I made friends with the boy across the street. We promised to write to each other during the winter. I did, but he didn't write back.

Papoo and I were best buddies. Every summer, he took me to the harness races at Ocean Downs, where I learned that a pacer wears a metal strap around its legs to ensure it maintains the smooth pacing gait. On the other hand, because the trotter has to lift its legs higher to trot, it does not wear the strap. I also learned that Papoo was right when he said "long odds" meant the horse would probably break its gait during the race. I put my two dollars on a pacer because when it won, those two dollars would become sixty, but it broke its gait around the first turn!

On my outings with Papoo, I did not notice that the silver flask was no longer stowed under the front seat of the car. I simply relished the fact that he was once again my favorite companion.

I also loved the King's Highway house. It had a secret—a fully enclosed stairway in the rear that descended from the master bedroom to the kitchen. Woo had explained that her bedroom at the top of those stairs used to be the maid's room. The stairs off the bedroom allowed the maid to get to the kitchen without disturbing the family.

"So Ada would have lived with us in the olden days? That would be wonderful!" I immediately imagined the sound of Ada's singing reverberating throughout the house day in and day out.

One morning when I bounced down the secret stairs to breakfast, I was stopped short by strange sounds. Not knowing why exactly, I tiptoed silently down the last few steps, opened the door oh, so slowly, and cautiously peered around the edge. Papoo was sitting at the kitchen table, crying; his head in his hands.

"I'm so sorry," Papoo sobbed. "I don't know what came over me. It won't happen again. I'll go back to AA straight away."

"Milton," Woo said in an icy voice. I was shocked. No one called Papoo Milton. I had even forgotten that was his real name. And the tone of Woo's voice was terrifying. I turned around, bolted up the stairs, and jumped back into bed where I stayed until Woo called me.

"Helen, why haven't you come down to breakfast? Hurry up now."

This time, I went down the front stairs. Usually when I walked down the grand front stairs, I imagined myself in a hoop dress like those I saw in prints on the wall in the Bethany cottage; this time, I just felt relief that I could avoid the gloomy back stairs. Papoo was nowhere to be seen when I entered the kitchen. When he came home in time for dinner, I was so relieved.

That summer, Marion was old enough to spend a week by herself with Woowoo and Papoo. They had picked me up in Bethany on one of their visits, and Mother and Daddy would take me home to Wilmington when they stopped to drop Marion off for her visit. As we walked to the car, all of a sudden, Marion's eyes filled with tears.

"I don't want to stay," she sobbed. "Take me home with you."

Instantly, I noticed stress on the faces of all the adults. I didn't want Woowoo and Papoo to be disappointed that Marion didn't want to stay with them, and I didn't like the thought that they might be mad at Marion for not wanting to stay.

"Marion, I'll stay with you," I said. "It's a lot of fun here. You'll see!"

"What a wonderful idea!" Mother said.

"Are you sure?" Woo asked. "It will be another ten days before Papoo can take the two of you home."

"Oh, yes," I replied, suddenly not so sure at all.

"Well, it's settled then," Mother said. "Dry your tears Marion; Helen will be here too. Why don't you two go in the house while we finish saying goodbye."

"Okay ...," Marion said softly. I took her hand, and we walked through the back door onto the screen porch ... but I knew it wasn't okay at all. We watched from the living room as the car drove by the front of the house, slowing down to make a turn. The pit in my stomach deepened as my body understood that I was not going home after all. Without thinking, I burst through the front door.

"Wait, wait!" I shouted. "I want to come with you!" But they didn't hear me.

I walked into the house and up the front stairs into our room, where Marion was sitting on her bed crying.

"I will tell Woo we have to go home," I said. Marion nodded.

I walked into the kitchen, where Woo was making supper. She took one look at me. "I knew this was a bad idea," she said with her lips pressed firmly together. "I will tell Empy to change his plans for his day off on Tuesday so he can take you home. You'll have to stay here tonight and tomorrow night. Can you manage that?"

"Yes," I murmured. "Thank you."

On Tuesday, Papoo took us home to Wilmington. None of us spoke a word during the two-hour drive. I felt such a surge of relief when we turned into the driveway, but also a new worry.

"I'm sorry," I said as we walked to the front door.

Papoo stopped, knelt down, and gave each of us a huge hug.

"I understand," he said. "Homesickness is just one of those things that comes over you. We'll try again next summer if you want to."

I hugged him back as hard as I could.

One Saturday morning that next spring, I was alone with Mother helping her fold laundry.

"Helen," she said, "I've been struggling about whether or not to tell you this, but I think you are old enough to hear it. And I know that you and Papoo have a special relationship."

My stomach clenched as she continued. "Papoo has cancer, and he will have a big operation to remove the tumor. After that, he will have special treatments to make sure the cancer doesn't come back."

"Will he be all right?" I pleaded.

"We hope so. The treatments will leave him very weak, and you may notice the change when you see him this summer."

So I will see him this summer, I thought. *That means everything will be fine.* And it was. Papoo was thin, but when had he not been thin? I put cancer out of my mind.

The summer of 1956 brought a complete change. Jessie and Empy had moved into their new house. No secret stairways here. Instead, the house had the conventional floor plan of a mid-fifties Cape: living room, dining area, kitchen, master bedroom, small second bedroom, and bathroom on the first floor; two bedrooms under the sloping roof on the second floor and a small bathroom with a stall shower, one of my favorite features. I imagined myself as the drummer in one of Mother's favorite string bands when the high water pressure caused the stream from the showerhead to reverberate as it struck the sides of the metal stall. I also loved the big bedroom upstairs with its four beds for me and my three sisters. Mine was tucked in an alcove under an eave and was the same antique bed I used to sleep in at home. All the beds had elaborate headboards which were perfect for playing telephone: string was extended from bed to bed where each sister had her own tin can receiver.

Woo was thrilled to have her own yard, and she made elaborate plans for a triangular-shaped flower garden. To bring it to life she had hired Freddy, a Negro man who dug the garden, planted it, and maintained it for the six years they owned the house. Freddy's wife Margaret helped Woo around the house. She knew how to make sweet pone, a special corn-based dish Woo had loved as a child, but never cooked herself. It took hours in a low oven sitting in a steam bath. I loved it too. Margaret also helped with Thanksgiving dinner just like Ada had. Woo and Papoo were thrilled to have a house big enough for all six of the Brookses to stay overnight.

I settled into a new, but still familiar routine during summer visits to the new house. I developed an affection for Freddy and Margaret—not as deep as my love for Ada, but a warm relationship nonetheless. I knew Woo liked them too, because she told me once that she had never expected to find anyone as reliable as Ada, but Freddy and Margaret came pretty close. I continued to see the summer friends whom I had met at the King's Highway house and continued to make new ones. Papoo changed jobs and now was head pharmacist at the pharmacy inside Beebe Hospital. I missed the old pharmacy a little bit, but now, as a teenager, I didn't revel in the visits as much as I once had. As far as I could tell, life in Lewes was comfortable and stable.

"Helen," Mother said on an April morning in 1962, "I have some bad news. Papoo is very, very sick with cancer. He wants us to bring you to Lewes on a special trip to buy you a high school graduation present."

"I don't understand," I said, confused. "I remember a few years ago that you told me Papoo had cancer, but he was treated and got better. No one has said anything since. He's fine!"

"We didn't see any reason to worry you. He has had some other treatments since ..."

"Is that why he has sometimes been so lethargic and withdrawn? He didn't even want to go to the races last summer!" I interrupted. "I've been telling myself it's just old age!"

"Yes. Last summer he was receiving treatment which really wore him out. And now the cancer is back again."

I was quiet. At first, I felt anger at the concealment, but all of a sudden I understood the implications of the end of the code of silence.

"You're telling me that he might not make my graduation, aren't you?"

"Yes. I'm so sorry."

When we arrived in Lewes, I was shocked by Papoo's appearance. He had always been lean and angular, but now he was gaunt and his skin was grey. He did not get up to embrace me, so I went to him and placed a gentle kiss on his cheek.

"After you get settled," he said, " we will head to the jewelry store. They know we are coming, and they have set aside a selection of watches for you to choose from."

"Papoo, thank you, but if you don't feel well, you don't have to come."

"Of course I'm coming. I want to see you pick it out."

Daddy held Papoo's arm as he walked to the car and then into the store. Mother and Woo stayed home. There were no other customers in the store; I later realized this had been arranged to give us privacy. Papoo leaned heavily on the counter as the jeweler brought out a tray of watches. I took them in slowly until Daddy prompted me:.

"Helen, do you see one you like?"

I realized I should not linger.

"This one," I said, pointing to a dainty 14-karat gold oval watch with three tiny petals at each edge. "How much is it?"

Helen, center, wearing gift from Papoo under her wrist corsage

"That one's $110," the jeweler replied. I was aghast.

"That's too much. How about ..."

"Please wrap it," Papoo said, "and send me the bill." I leaned over and kissed him again.

On the way back to the car, as a wave of pain washed over him, Papoo suddenly collapsed, gasping and clinging to a parking meter. Daddy caught him just before he sunk down to the sidewalk. I understood that this outing had cost Papoo every ounce of strength he had. I could not hold back my tears.

Papoo died two weeks later. Although I felt skittish about my first encounter with death, I resolved to attend the funeral. However, Mother told me no; she and Daddy had decided that it was best for me to stay home. I could help Ada with the routines for my sisters while they were away. I did not protest, feeling a mixture of guilt and relief.

Shockingly, Papoo's sister Tense died in the Lewes house early in the morning after the funeral. Mother had been in the big room upstairs when she heard what she called "the death rattle" from Tense in the room across the hall. I shuddered at this news, wondering what a death rattle sounded like. I was doubly relieved that I had stayed home.

Two weeks after that, I was a member of the annual May Court, the spring version of the Homecoming Queen and her court. As I walked down the aisle under the ballon arch in the high school gym, I kept the fingers of my right hand, hidden under my wrist bouquet, on the face of the watch that I wore on my left wrist. How I wished that Papoo was standing among the proud parents and grandparents who lined the aisle.

24

Woo, Ada, and Me

When I was a little girl, Ada, who had worked for Woo when Mother was growing up and now worked for us, was one of five caring adults in my life —the equal of my parents and grandparents. Like all adults, she knew everything. But every now and then, she would befuddle me. One day, I burst into the kitchen where she was ironing and excitedly asked her to say a sentence in French. I had just read something that had led me to realize English isn't the only language in the world, and I couldn't wait to hear a demonstration. Ada was the nearest adult to ask, but she confused me when she said "I don't know no French."

"You don't?" I asked in amazement.

She hung her head and said "No." I had done something terribly wrong by asking, but what? I had hurt her feelings, but how? I slunk away.

Another time, my sisters and I were playing on the beach while Ada sat in her uniform on a bench on the boardwalk. She had accompanied us to the Bethany cottage, and this morning she was supervising our beach play until our parents arrived and we could go in the ocean. "Come down here and play with us," I called. She kept refusing, and I kept demanding until I realized I was creating a scene that was embarrassing her. I turned away, annoyed at her stubbornness.

Yet another time, something had aroused my curiosity about Ada's family, and I peppered my mother with questions:

"Where does she live?" I asked.

"Why do her grandchildren live with her?"

"Where is their mother?"

"Who is her husband?"

I was beginning to worry that her devotion to us cheated her own family.

"Ada doesn't have a husband," my mother said. "And I don't know where their mother is. That's enough questions." There was an air of the forbidden in her voice.

So every family is not like ours? But what are other families like? And why can't I know?

None of these incidents marred my love for Ada in any way. I looked forward to Tuesdays when she came to iron, and Fridays when she came to clean. She was cheerful and upbeat, always greeting me with a hug. I loved inhaling her sweet scent, and I loved listening to her sing as she worked. Tuesdays when she ironed were better than Fridays when the vacuum cleaner drowned out her singing.

Most of all, I loved her stories. Some were about Mother as a little girl, reading curled up under the dining room table as Ada bustled about. Some were about us when we were babies. A favorite was about the time she caught one of us as we rolled off the changing table. Perhaps the best one was the time she wildly flagged down the bus with a garment pulled from her bag in haste—it turned out to be her underwear! She loved to describe the embarrassment of the driver when she said "What? Ain't you ever seen a lady's drawers before? Now ain't that too bad!"

In 1956, when I was eleven, we moved to a new house. The small brick colonial into which my parents had moved as newlyweds in 1941 was now too small for our family of four girls—and, besides, this was my mother's dream house. Located a short bus ride from downtown Wilmington, the brick colonial had been easily accessible for Ada. The new house was located far outside of town in a newly developed rural area, now requiring two bus rides and then a long drive from the end of the line to the house. She kept coming, but the rhythm changed. I wasn't there when she arrived and often not when she left.

On those afternoons when I was home, I stopped paying attention as Ada worked. I noticed she didn't sing as often, and she frequently had a rag pinned around her head, which we knew to be the sign of a headache. She seemed thinner and her face was frequently drawn. There were many steps to haul the vacuum cleaner up and down. I wish I had carried it for her now and then, but I didn't.

Years passed and I had earned a driver's license. Occasionally my mother would ask me to drive Ada to the bus stop. One cold winter afternoon as I drove us along the country road, I was struck by the harshness of her commute way out from the center of Wilmington. On cold winter afternoons like this one, when darkness arrived early, the entire journey was bleak.

"Let me take you all the way home, Ada," I pleaded. "I don't want to leave you here. It's cold and you are the only person waiting. What if the bus doesn't come?"

She wouldn't hear of it. "It always comes," she said.

"Do you have a dime for a phone call if it doesn't?" I asked.

"Yes. You go on now."

I complied, but I was plagued by worry as I looked at the forlorn figure hunched under the streetlamp receding in the rearview mirror.

One Christmas, I drove to Ada's house to pick her up. She always cooked Christmas dinner for us. I was pleased to be admitted to her small row house on A Street in the Black section of town. Small but neat, her house smelled sweet, just like she did. Marvin and Marsha, her grandchildren, smiled down from photographs on the wall. Dusty, our rejected cocker spaniel whom Ada had rescued when we were about to take him to the pound as punishment for humping the cats at the front door one too many times, bounded up from the cellar.

"Dusty!" I exclaimed. "I can't believe you haven't been run over yet." Dusty was not known for obeying commands.

"Oh, we don't let him out," Ada said. "He goes in the cellar." I tried not to think about that.

On this particular Christmas, about 1964, Mother had told me we didn't have enough butter and asked me to see if Ada had some. She didn't, but she said we could stop at the corner store, which was open despite the holiday.

"You let me do the talking," she said.

As we walked in, conversation stopped. I felt electricity in the air. Ada greeted everyone in her cheeriest voice, and said, "We here need a pound of butter." The person behind the counter hesitated, and I wondered for a fleeting second if she would refuse to sell it to us.

"That'll be five dollars," the counter person said.

"That's too high," Ada began, but I stopped her.

"That's just fine. Thank you very much." We stood in tense silence while the counter person wrapped the butter.

Outside, Ada was furious. "Those uppity folks. They don't have no manners," she said. And I realized that all the trouble in Alabama and Mississippi was dividing Negro people as well as Whites.

Another day when home from college and lounging in the kitchen to talk to my mother, I noticed a check for Ada made out by my father. I idly picked it up and turned it over to see an "X" on the back along with my father's signature below it.

Thunderstruck, I blurted out to my mother, "Doesn't Ada know how to read and write?"

"No, of course not. I thought you knew that," she replied.

Know that. How could I know that? You wouldn't ever answer my questions, I silently accused her.

I walked out of the room to be with my feelings. I thought of the two Black women newly admitted to my southern women's college, the first of their race to attend. I thought of Sally and Maud, the maids who cleaned our dorm, and whom I had befriended as surrogate Adas in my home away from home. Again, I thought of all the trouble in Mississippi and Alabama. And I was angry.

Years passed. I graduated from college, married, then moved to Connecticut. Ada had attended my wedding (but not the reception). However, she usually wasn't at my parents' home in Delaware when I visited. I was young, immersed in my new adult life, unconsciously assuming that the lives of my loved ones continued as they always had. But one day, about a decade after my wedding, I answered the phone to hear Woo telling me unbelievable news. Ada had died; her funeral was in two days.

"She died?!" I exclaimed. "How could I not know that she was even sick?! Why didn't you alert me?"

"Really, Helen, I didn't know either. How could I? Since Helen and Dick moved to Hawaii, we don't see Ada any more."

That's right, I murmured to myself. *Ada had slipped from my sight. How did I allow that to happen?*

Out loud, I said, "I'm sorry. You're right, but of course we will go to the funeral. I'll get in touch with my sisters, and we'll make a plan to pick you up."

"You can't be serious," she said.

"Ada worked for my family for thirty years, and for yours for I don't know how long prior to that. She has been a part of our family forever. How could you not go? It's disrespectful." Sullenly, she agreed to go.

At the church, Woo, my sisters, and I sat in the third row on the right. We could see into the coffin. Ada was dressed all in white. Curious, I thought.

A door next to the altar opened and a long line of women attired in white dresses, hats, and gloves silently filed in and encircled the coffin. They joined hands, raised them in unison, and burst into glorious song. Ada's sisters were celebrating her life and mourning her death. The hair raised on the back of my neck. I wept.

Woo recoiled. She moved restlessly in her seat, becoming increasingly agitated. All of sudden, I realized what a mistake I had made to insist that she come. This was a cultural clash she could not endure. My grandmother sitting in the pew

Ada at Jessie's wedding 1970

near me was the same woman who had exclaimed shrilly one day as I drove her through town, "Don't turn there. That's n..... street." She was the same woman born in 1892 who had grown up on the Eastern Shore of Maryland at the height of Jim Crow. The same woman whose own mother, the first Helen, had died in the early 1950s in her nineties, meaning she must have been born when the Civil War was blazing. I knew the family had owned slaves.

Sister Jessie, her namesake, noticed her agitation too. "We need to take her out," I whispered. "You're nearer to the end; can you do it?" Jessie nodded, and they rose. I could not bear to turn and watch the reaction of the sea of Black faces to the abrupt departure of two White ones. I shrank back into my seat, humiliated by the disruption we were causing, and enraged at myself for being so obtuse.

As we exited the church, I nervously scanned for Lucille,

Ada's niece, who had invited us to the post-funeral supper. I avoided eye contact with everyone else, on guard against expressions of hostility that I dreaded, but thought we deserved. We met at the door where she must have been waiting for me. "I don't think you should come to the supper," she said immediately.

"I know. I don't think that we should come either. I am so sorry, and I apologize for my grandmother."

Lucille nodded.

"Thank you for contacting us. I hope you don't regret it. We loved Ada, and I was honored to be here."

I think, I hope, that Lucille said, "It was important for you to come."

As we drove in stony silence back to Woo's apartment, I was even angrier than I had been years before when I had stumbled on the fact that Ada was illiterate. Then I had been angry at Mother; now I was angry at Woo. How could she behave so abominably? She, a woman who had had close relationships with many Black people over her entire life—Mozelle, Floyd, Freddy and Margaret, and Ada. She, who had been so proud of Judy Johnson, the Black baseball player from Snow Hill now enshrined in the Negro League Baseball Hall of Fame. Ada had practically raised her daughter, for heaven's sake, and was a huge presence in her granddaughters' lives. Yet Woo couldn't sit respectfully for one hour to honor a woman who had served her and her family for over fifty years? I mentally rehearsed a speech that she deserved—a speech that would deliver the condemnation of her outrageous behavior.

I glanced over at Woo in the passenger seat next to me.

Her jaw was clenched, her gnarled hands were balled into tight fists in her lap, and she sat as erect as her osteoporosis would allow. Her entire body dared me to assault her. I couldn't do it.

"Woo, we will see you into your apartment, and then we will head back to Connecticut."

"That's fine," she said. My sisters said nothing.

On the drive back to Connecticut, Marion exploded. "How could she?! I've never been so humiliated in my life. What did she say when you took her out, Jessie?"

"She said, 'What kind of nonsense was that? You'd think they would have learned by now! It made my skin crawl!'"

Suddenly, I felt profoundly sad. Marion, Jessie, and I lived in the contemporary world, but Woo was trapped in an earlier time. We felt grief for the loss of our beloved Ada, but Woo could not express any feeling for a woman she had known intimately for decades. Such a loss.

25

Woo, the Aunts, and Me

Beyond my parents and grandparents, Ada was the most important, but not the only important, adult in my life. Woo's three sisters, Helen (Aunt Helen), Mary (Nanny), and Eva (Beba), played significant roles as well. During my childhood, they lived together in a two-bedroom apartment in Philadelphia with their mother, my great-grandmother, the first Helen.

The elevator was my favorite part of a childhood visit to the Aunts. A dignified, uniformed Negro gentleman stood by the open elevator door as we entered the lobby. The six of us—Mother, Daddy, my three sisters, and I—barely fit into the mahogany-paneled elevator with just enough room to spare for the operator. He reached out a white-gloved hand to pull a grate across the opening and then a lever that shut the heavy doors. Daddy would say, "The Townsends, please," to which the operator replied "Yessir." He turned a large dial clockwise, and that started the elevator moving up. He dialed back slowly as we approached the Aunts' floor until we came to a stop. When he opened the heavy doors, he would check to make sure that the floor of the elevator was perfectly aligned with the hallway floor. If not, he would nudge the dial so the elevator moved the tiniest bit. Then he would open the grate to let us out. I tried very hard not to look down into the crack between the elevator and the hall floor, but I inevitably glanced at the yawning cavern visible as I stepped across.

Safely across the crack, I steeled myself to confront the bear who awaited us just inside the apartment door. About three feet high standing on his hind legs, he had an open mouth full of teeth and long claws on his front paws. When I was very young, he also stared me directly in the eye. The fact that umbrellas sat in the tray between his hind feet did not comfort me one bit.

Once the entrance hallway greetings were over, and we could escape from the bear, the apartment became a novel playground. Immediately to the right of the front door was a long, dark hall, perfect for chasing one another. It landed us in the kitchen, where a maid and the aromas of dinner greeted us. When we made the return run down the hallway, sprinting across the entrance hall past the bear, we landed in one of the two large bedrooms with a fascinating view of the city. Cars were so little, and people—just specks down there on the street. Slowly, I realized that the long hall existed so that the maid could walk from the kitchen to answer the front door without having to pass through the living room. Only later did I come to understand that the maid did not disappear like the Tooth Fairy; rather, she left by the back stairs and went down to the alley, past the garbage cans, and then out to the street.

Sometimes these family trips to see the Aunts included a trip to the Philadelphia Art Museum, where I was mesmerized by classical sculpture and medieval armor. Later, I took the train from Wilmington to Philadelphia on my own to be greeted by an aunt with tickets to the Ice Capades. Great-grandmother had died by then, freeing a bed for an overnight stay. When my college friends and I visited, we spent hours trying on clothes in Wanamaker's Department Store. These shopping trips, which were always punctuated by an elegant lunch in a dining room with white tablecloths and more Negro people in uniforms.

In addition to Woo's sisters, I had a "bonus" aunt and uncle who lived next door to us in Edgemoor Terrace. Although they were not related to us, they were practically members of the family whom we called Aunt Helena and Uncle Bill. As far as I knew, they had no children, and evidently no nieces or nephews either, so they adopted us. Every other fall they teamed up with Mother and Daddy to host the World-Famous Oyster Roast. With food and drinks spread across our neighboring two yards on what was inevitably a beautiful October Saturday, guests and their children streamed in and out all day. For this one special day, we kids could run with abandon through Aunt Helena's yard; it was strictly off limits every other day. I did try to sneak through on the way to my friend Barbara's on other days, but invariably I would hear a firm rap on the window and Aunt Helena's scolding voice: "Helen, you know better!"

Each year, I watched with fascination as Daddy and then Uncle Bill expertly shucked oysters, but nothing could entice me to eat one of those slimy things. Nor would I try the oyster stew that Ada made just the way Woo liked it. One time I did sneak a bite out of a stunning Red Delicious apple sitting in a fruit bowl while I was awaiting the party. To my surprise and relief, no one accused me—or any of my sisters. I guess Mother was too busy to pursue a petty criminal.

Every Christmas Day, Daddy would make the hour drive through smelly, industrial Marcus Hook to bring the Aunts to our house for the holiday meal. Once we all got home, Aunt Helena and Uncle Bill joined us too. We children eagerly anticipated a second round of gifts once they arrived. We all knew that Beba would sit next to Daddy as he carved the turkey and reach for the pope's nose. We also knew that he would scold her, saying, "Eva, one year this knife will slip and you will lose a finger!" Ada would say, "Miss Mary (or Miss Eva or Miss Helen), can I serve you some mashed potatoes?" which slowly taught me that my aunts had known Ada for a long time. Gradually I came to understand what an effort Daddy exerted to make this two-hour roundtrip twice on the same day after he had been up early to make buckwheat pancakes for Christmas breakfast and to complete the egg nog, which had been fermenting overnight. Even though I often became car sick, particularly in Marcus Hook, I began to accompany him on the first trip because he deserved a companion.

Woo rarely accompanied us on the trips to Philadelphia, but she and Papoo were always present for the holidays. As their adult conversation seeped into me over the years, I came to understand that Aunt Helen had played a significant role in Woo's life, and that she had endured tragedy in her own. I was not surprised when Mother told me that Aunt Helen wanted me to have her silver, which had been made by the Stieff Silver Company in Baltimore. On Christmas Day 1965, I was newly engaged. I thought I knew what I would see when I opened the chest Aunt Helen presented to me, but I was taken aback by the place settings for twelve, including ice cream forks, ice tea spoons, and an asparagus server. As I turned over the teaspoons, I noticed that some were engraved *HTW* while others were engraved *HTS* for the Helen Townsend Stabler I knew.

"Aunt Helen," I asked, "why do some of these spoons have a *W* engraved on them?"

"They're from my first marriage to Eric Wiseheart," she replied. "He was a wonderful doctor who helped Empy begin his career in pharmacy."

She stopped speaking abruptly, and all the adults were quiet. After a beat or two, I said, "Thank you for this beautiful gift; I will take care of every piece forever."

"You're welcome. Now it's Marion's turn to open a present."

Later that night Mother told me, "Eric died in the first year of their marriage, and, years later, Caleb Stabler died in the first year of their marriage as well!"

I could think of no response to that other than to double down in my heart on my promise to treasure the silver forever.

That spring, Aunt Helena, our former neighbor and co-host of the World-Famous Oyster Roast, made a special trip to see me when I was home from college for vacation. By that time, we had moved across town from Edgemoor Terrace, and I rarely saw her.

"Why is she making a special trip?" I asked Mother, feeling a bit annoyed because I had had to postpone plans to be home for her visit.

"You'll see," Mother replied mysteriously.

Aunt Helena walked in with a large package wrapped in wedding paper.

"I wanted to give this to you myself," she said, "in a private moment before all the festivities around the wedding begin."

I took the package. "Please open it."

Inside was a large linen tablecloth trimmed with lace around the hem and meticulously cross-stitched with a charming country scene around the border.

"I made it for Edwin and his fiancée, but he didn't come home. I want you to have it."

In a flash, I understood. Edwin must be the handsome young man in military dress whose photograph I had seen many times in Aunt Helena and Uncle Bill's living room. He was their son, and he had lost his life in World War II. Here was another gift of love. I rose to embrace Aunt Helena.

"I am so honored. Every time I use it, I will think of Edwin and you and Uncle Bill. Thank you so very much."

After Aunt Helena departed, I took the tablecloth into the room where my wedding gifts were laid out, carefully draping it over the back of the sofa so that the corner embroidered *1938* was displayed. I lingered a moment to regard the silver chest propped open and felt a surge of obligation to the women who had entrusted me with such significant treasures from their lives. I made a vow to pass on these precious items and the stories attached to them to women of the next generation, should the future present me with the opportunity.

On July 9, 1966, sitting at the head table at my wedding

Beba, Aunt Helen and Woo at Helen's wedding, 1966;
Mary and Emily not in photo

reception, I looked over to the table where Woo, her sisters, and a cousin sat ramrod straight. Aunt Helen, Beba (Eva), Nanny (Mary), and cousin Emily, Uncle Charles's widow, were dressed as if they were members of the same tribe—as in fact, they were. Each wore a lace dress over a matching taffeta slip, color-coordinated hat, shoes, and clutch purse. Each had emerged from a recent beauty parlor visit with newly permed hair and carefully buffed nails. They sat regally, with upright posture. The passing of decades had not eroded their sense of social status developed as children in the halcyon days of Snow Hill.

Now in their eighties, with not a child among them, in their dotages a decade hence, her sisters would become Woo's responsibility; she would resent this bitterly. One by one, she found institutions for them, where she rarely visited. She would be in her eighties herself when responsibility for her sisters arrived on her doorstep. They needed her, their younger sister, as she had needed them decades before. In contrast to how they assisted her, she fulfilled her obligations to them grudgingly.

Aunt Helen ended up in the Smyrna Home for the Blind.

"It's a blessing, Helen," Woo told me in one phone call. "They usually only take residents of Delaware, and of course they lived in Philadelphia. But I told the woman about our deep roots in Wilmington, and she agreed that it qualified her! The state will pay all of her expenses. What a relief!"

That summer, Joe, my first husband, and I stopped to see Aunt Helen on the way to our annual vacation in Bethany. As we entered her room, the nurses were struggling to get her to sit down in an armchair. Her resistance was fierce and futile as they forced her into a sitting position.

"No ties, no ties!" she screamed, flailing her bony arms as a nurse wound sturdy canvas ropes around her, binding her to the back of the chair.

"She will fall out if we don't restrain her, and she will get bed sores if we leave her in bed," the nurse explained as she left. "I'm sorry you had to see that."

"Aunt Helen, it's Helen," I said through the lump in my throat, forcing myself to stroke her hand.

"No ties!" she screamed again, straining against the straps that bound her.

I stepped back. She quieted and her chin dropped to her chest.

I looked at Joe, who nodded. We left. When we encountered her nurse in the hall, I said, "Our presence seems to agitate my aunt further. We think it's best to leave."

"Yes," the nurse replied. "I understand."

I called Woo when we reached Bethany.

"We just had the most horrific visit with Aunt Helen. They have to restrain her, and she hates it. She screams and struggles."

"Why do you think I don't go? I almost suggested that you not visit, but I thought you wouldn't believe me unless you saw the situation for yourself."

"Can't something be done to relieve her suffering?"

"Do you want to take responsibility for her? I've done the best I could," she replied.

I didn't. And so it was with a mixture of guilt and relief that I received the news of her death a few months later. Woo arranged for her burial near Kate in the cemetery in Snow Hill.

Beba (Eva) fared better. For several years, she lived alone in a little apartment on Ironshire Street, near the Nassawango Country Club on the Pocomoke River in Snow Hill. A few old friends still visited her. Each summer, she would arrange for Joe and me to play golf at the Club and then meet us for lunch. She adored Joe and was very proud to encourage him to order what she knew to be the best crab cakes on the Eastern Shore. I didn't need additional encouragement to order them too.

By the time she was in a nursing home in Salisbury, Joe and I were divorced; I had married Dick, and Katie was a year old. Like Joe, Dick was gracious about visiting a very old lady, even one he had never met. "Katie is the fifth generation," I told him. "I feel a deep obligation to arrange for Beba to see Katie." When we arrived, I placed Katie on the bed next to Beba, who reached out a hand to touch her. Katie allowed it, and Beba smiled. This time when I received news of the death, I felt gratitude that I had done the right thing.

To my shame—and Woo's—I do not know Nanny's (Mary's) story. I didn't ask, and she didn't tell me until she reported in one phone call that Nanny was buried in Snow Hill too.

Sometime in the late eighties, when Dick, Katie, and I were vacationing in Bethany, we took a field trip to the cemetery in Snow Hill. Woo had recently died and was buried in Parksley, Virginia, with Papoo and his parents. With the passing of the last of that generation, I was overcome with the desire to visit them. And there they were: Mother, Father, Kate, and Jim, baby Robley, Helen, Mary, and generations that go even further back into the eighteenth century. All had appropriate headstones, although none were as elaborate as Kate's. With a start, I realized I couldn't find Beba. I knew she was there, but where? A search revealed a small grey, malleable metal tag on a short stake: *Eva S. Townsend, 1888 - 1983,* the letters flattened almost into obscurity.

Back in Bethany, I called my sister Jessie, full of indignation. "Beba doesn't have a headstone," I fumed. "Why would Woo do that?"

"She doesn't?!" Jessie replied, to my great satisfaction, sounding equally appalled. "I think she got very tired of caring for her sisters at the end and had just run out of steam by the time Beba died. I'll take care of it."

And she did. Today you will find six of the eight children

in the Methodist cemetery in Snow Hill. The oldest son, Charles, is with his wife's family, the Joneses—Mother's family of origin. The eighth, Jessie, lies in Parksley, Virginia, with Empy, her ticket out into the world, but the other six have returned to where they began.

2.6

Woo, Husbands, and Me

Woo lived long enough to become a great-grandmother, although it took me two marriages to present her with her great-granddaughter Katherine, called Katie, in honor of Woo's beloved sister.

My first husband, Joe

I stood at the window of my empty dorm room looking out past the magnolia tree, across the green expanse of the front campus to the red brick wall that separated this haven from the world. Commencement had concluded. My roommate, her parents, and my parents had already departed. College was really over.

My roving gaze caught the little red and white Chevy Nova waiting for me at the curb of the drive leading through the gate in the red brick wall up to the front porch of Main Hall where I had lived senior year. It was Woo's car. She had given it to Joe and me as a combination graduation/wedding present. I was driving it back home to Wilmington, where I would await my wedding day about a month away.

I had very mixed feelings about all of it. For one thing, when I had asked Woo what kind of car she would get next, she had shocked me by saying, "None."

"You're giving up driving?" I had asked incredulously. "You're only 73. You can drive for years and years yet!"

"Maybe, but now that I've moved downtown, I can easily use the bus, have things delivered, and be free of the hassle of finding on-street parking each time I go out. And Dick will come get me to visit you all."

"That's why I didn't think you should have moved to the Mayfair," I said with a tone of exasperation. "No parking."

"I really like being back in the old neighborhood," she replied with a slight catch in her voice. "It brings back memories."

"I see." Nonetheless, I still felt that the universe had shifted a bit in the wrong direction. I reassured myself—seventy-three is not old at all. The fact that Woo has decided not to drive anymore is just a lifestyle change, nothing more.

My mind drifted to the first time Woo met Joe, my fiancé, two years earlier. After Papoo had died, Woo had sold their house in Lewes and taken a garden apartment on the outskirts of Wilmington. In August 1964, prior to my junior year at Randolph-Macon Woman's College, I drove straight there from Chapel Hill, North Carolina, where I had spent a very sweaty summer taking calculus and physics to prepare for my upcoming chemistry major. I had declared my major at the very last minute the previous spring without having followed the preparatory curriculum for science majors. As a result, I had gaps to fill before diving into advanced chemistry courses.

I recall sitting in the driveway of Woo's building, gathering resolve to knock on the door. For some reason that I can't recall, behind that door Joe was waiting. It seems preposterous that we would have arranged for them to meet without my being present, but we did. How she would react to this Italian/Ukrainian Catholic son of a blue-collar laborer, I did not know. I did know that a very snobby, patrician daughter of the Eastern Shore of Maryland could be expected to react badly. It would help, however, that he was very handsome.

Woo wasn't my only worry. Although I wore my diamond ring all summer, its presence didn't stop men from flirting with me, or me with them. In fact, I came very close to a disastrous move. Joe had written passionate letters almost daily all summer, but I hadn't kept up that pace—or tone—in return. I was feeling guilty and confused.

Joe opened the door, sweeping me into an embrace as I knew he would. I was embarrassed to see Woo in the background.

"I've missed you so much!"

"Well, I'm here now," I replied as I stepped back, releasing myself from his arms. "I see you have met Woo."

At the mention of her name, Woo spoke up. "Joe and I have had the best visit. He sang "Ave Maria" for me. He has such a beautiful tenor voice! And he was so interested to hear about how I used to sing and act."

Well, I thought, he has charmed her. *One worry assuaged at least.*

"I'm so glad," I said.

Two years had passed; my chemistry major was completed, and my marriage to Joe was imminent. But I seemed hesitant to move on. All of a sudden, Maud's voice snapped me out of my reverie. Maud was my favorite of all the maids who served in the dorms.

"Oh, Miss Helen. I thought you's gone. I'll come back."

"No, no, the car is packed; I was just taking one more look around."

"Yes, ma'am. I knows it's hard to leave. We will love the new girls, but we will always love you too."

I resisted giving her a hug, picked up my last bag, and walked reluctantly out of what had been my room.

On a perfect summer day in early July 1966, I married Joe. We had a tumultuous honeymoon in Europe with ongoing arguments about when to stop for the day, where to eat, and what routes to take as we drove from Greece to Scotland over the course of six weeks. *Have I made a terrible mistake*? I kept asking myself. I couldn't wait to get home to begin a life with some predictable structure. *Things will be better,* I reassured myself, *once he starts his job and I get immersed in my MAT program.*

By the next spring, I felt on solid enough ground to invite Woo for a visit. She had found a driver who would take her to catch a train at the Wilmington Station, and I would pick her up in New Haven in the little red and white Chevy Nova. As we whizzed up Interstate 91 past an eighteen wheeler with the windows open in these days before air conditioning, she shouted over the road noise, "Helen, you're such a good driver!"

"What?" I asked, rolling the windows up.

"You're such a good driver. I wouldn't know what to do about these trucks, but I feel very safe with you," she repeated. "I'm really glad I gave you the car."

"Well, thank you again. It knows this route by heart since I've been commuting from Hartford to New Haven three days each week since the fall." *I guess highway driving can be intimidating,* I thought. *Maybe that's why she didn't want to drive anymore. She never did drive at 60 mph,* I guess.

"Yes, I know you're going to be a very good teacher when you get your degree. The school that gets you will be very lucky indeed."

I felt the little surge of confidence that she always evoked with her frequent praise. In her eyes, I knew I could just about walk on water.

The next time she visited, we traveled to Joe's parents' house for Sunday dinner. Afterward, they would take her to the train station for the trip home because their house was nearer to New Haven than our house. It was spring again, and, in fact, the day that the clocks sprang ahead. We had discussed this, and she was certain she had the correct departure time. However, the phone was ringing when we walked into our house after a one-hour return drive. It was Joe's father.

"Mrs. Lewis had the time wrong," he said. "The train had already departed when we got there. We have rebooked her. She will spend the night at Aunt Delia's, and we will take her to the station again tomorrow."

"I'm so sorry. We would offer to come get her and take her to the train ourselves, but we both have to work. And so do you!"

"Yes," Joe's father said, "but Julia doesn't. She'll take her."

"Thank you so much. I apologize for the confusion."

After hanging up the phone, I said to Joe, "Woo seems more easily confused these days." He nodded.

There would be one more visit from Woo to Joe and me. I arrived home from school one afternoon to notice the ironing board set up in the kitchen.

"Hi. I see you ironed something today."

"Well, I tried to," she replied, "but the iron just wouldn't heat up!"

"I'll check it for you." I walked into the kitchen to see the hand mixer, without beaters, plugged into the wall and sitting on the ironing board. I put it away quietly and retrieved the iron from the same cabinet.

"It seems to be working all right now," I said. "Would you still like to use it?"

She walked into the kitchen, looking more bent over than I remembered.

"Yes, I want to wear this blouse back on the train tomorrow. Is it set to cotton?"

"Yes," I said as I adjusted the controls. "I'll just do some preparations for dinner here in the kitchen while you iron. Then I can put everything away for you."

She didn't answer, as she was focused on her ironing.

The next evening, I called her.

"Hi. I just wanted to make sure you got home safely."

"Of course," she said brusquely. "Why wouldn't I? Norman was right there waiting for me."

"Good," I replied.

Next I dialed my father.

"Daddy, I'm worried about Woo. I don't think she should visit Joe and me by train again, and I'm concerned that she may not be managing all right on her own at home.

Daddy listened quietly while I recounted the ironing story. As I concluded, he said, "Your mother and I have been wondering too. You may not know that I have been handling her affairs for a while now, and we have seen little signs of decline as well. I'm going to see what our alternatives are."

"I'm so relieved, Daddy. I don't want anything to happen to her!"

Six months later, Joe and I were driving to Wilmington to help move Woo into Ingleside, an assisted living facility. I had expected her to be defiant or at least resistant, but she surprised me.

"Helena and Bill live there," she told me. "I haven't seen much of them since they lived next to you girls when you were growing up. And Lura and Ruth Cann. And I understand the food is excellent."

So this is just like the car, I thought. She knows the time has come, so she's making the best of it. She can be very difficult in many situations, but she is aging gracefully. I hope I can remember this when my turn comes.

I was surprised by how much the move exhausted her. As we exited the elevator with a last load, she banged precious ceramic lamp shades hard against the frame. She had insisted that she carry them personally so she could ensure that they were moved safely.

"The shades!" I cried out without thinking.

"I'm just so tired ...," her voice trailed off, and her hands, barely grasping the shades, dangled at her sides. Joe dropped his box and swooped to rescue them. *He is a good person,* I reminded myself.

On the drive back to Connecticut, Joe and I had very little to say to one another. Our marriage was disintegrating. For years, I had done my best to support and encourage him. He had graduated absolutely last in his law school class and failed the bar exam. I kept assuring him that those details didn't matter. After all, he had a good job at the bank, and he could just leave law school behind. However, as the years slipped by, everyone in his cohort at the bank and his best friend from undergraduate school, who worked at a different bank—everyone—had been promoted to bank officer. Some had been promoted twice. And, in contrast to his career, mine was prospering. I had earned a sixth year certificate in education that qualified me as an administrator in Connecticut, and I had an exciting new job as a high school assistant principal. My colleagues—all male—loved me, including Dick Regan, Chair of the Science Department, with whom I worked closely.

Furthermore, everyone had children but Joe and me. It had been very hard to perform when the thermometer said we should. Finally, I had suggested that we consult a doctor who had advised that we check outside plumbing first. The results were in—maybe a dozen live sperm were where there should have been tens of thousands, which meant that children were not in the cards for us. The news had split me wide open. *Why am I doing this?* I asked myself. Impulsively, I asked Joe for a divorce, but, then terrified, pulled back immediately. We both knew we were on thin ice.

A few months later, I was on the phone to Woo from my new apartment.

"I have some bad news," I said.

"What?" she asked with concern.

"Joe and I have separated. We are getting a divorce." I waited, feeling like I did years before when I had broken a treasured tea cup. Then and now, she surprised me. She forgave me instantly for breaking the tea cup, and now she said,

"I could see you were not happy. Joe just couldn't keep up. He is a very nice man, but that's not enough. I am very sorry—I know you have broken his heart, and I know that makes you sorry too. But I understand."

Through tears I said, "Thank you so much. There is a note in the mail with my new address and phone number."

My second husband, Dick

Not long after my divorce, Dick Regan was divorced too. After seven years of a strictly professional relationship, to our mutual astonishment, we fell in love and married. Like Joe, Dick embraced Woo. Over several years he drove five hours from Connecticut to Delaware to pick her up for visits. The last one occurred in the summer of 1981 when Katie, Woo's first great-grandchild, was an infant. I have a treasured photograph of Katie in Woo's lap, almost slipping out of her grasp just like the ceramic lamp shades. Now 89, Woo was very frail; her gnarled hands held the baby with difficulty. Dick, who was working at a camp that summer, called to tell me he had forgotten his supper. It would take me forty-five minutes to drive the round trip to the camp. Did I dare?

I put Katie in her crib, and, with my throat in my mouth, I said to Woo, "I'm going to take Dick's supper to him. If the baby cries, you can sing to her like you used to do for us, but don't pick her up."

To my great relief, Woo assured me immediately when I returned home: "The baby didn't make a peep."

A few years later, as her health continued to decline, we all agreed that Woo needed to be near family so we could see her and be in touch with her doctors. Mother and Daddy now lived in Hawaii so my sister Jessie, who lived in Pittsburgh, stepped in. Woo moved to a nursing home near Jessie's home. Dick encouraged me to go. "Woo is very old," he said. "You don't know how much time she has left. You two are very close; I know a visit from you would brighten her life considerably. Katie and I will be fine while you're away."

"Thank you for understanding. You have been so supportive of her and me."

And so I visited Woo once in Pittsburgh. I was overcome when I walked into her room. At Ingleside, she'd had a semblance of a home, with a bedroom separate from her living room and a small kitchen. Here she had a hospital room: a bed, a rolling bedside table, and a chair covered with serviceable aqua vinyl filled the small space. So small, she was sitting in the chair looking out the window, dressed, as always, to the nines. She may have lost her furniture, but she had kept her wardrobe, and she was ready for dinner out with her oldest granddaughter. I swallowed the lump in my throat.

"Hi, Woo," I called out cheerfully. "You look lovely."

She struggled to get up, but something told me not to help.

"Well, there you are. I'm hungry for some decent food!"

Oh, oh, I thought.

"Okay, let's go. I've made reservations at a restaurant Jessie tells me is superb!"

As we walked down the hall, she held the railing, and then suddenly stopped. Inhaling deeply, she tried to straighten up, but she could not hold the position.

"My back," she exclaimed. "If it would just stop hurting ...,"

I took her arm as she folded over again, with her head thrust forward just barely reaching my shoulder.

A few weeks after that, Jessie called me.

"Woo will be having abdominal surgery tomorrow. They think there's an obstruction."

"Oh, Jessie," I said tearfully.

"I know. Don't say it."

Two days later, I called Woo. The phone rattled as she tried to pick it up. I was afraid she would drop it.

"How are you?"

Clearly annoyed, she said, "I don't know what's wrong with those doctors. I'm still not right!"

Jessie called a few days later to tell me that Woo had died. Once again, Dick lent me the support and understanding I needed. "Katie is too young to attend Woo's funeral," he said. "You go and be with your sisters. We will be here when you return."

"Did I ever tell you that Woo often told me what a kind and decent man she thinks you are?"

Dick, not known for easy expression of emotion, glanced away. "I'll miss her," he said.

At the funeral home in Parksley, Virginia, she lay regal in her casket. I stroked her forehead and her hair. At the cemetery, her headstone, already engraved, read *Jessie T. Lewis, 1892-1987*. Next to it, the headstone read *Milton P. Lewis, 1898-1962*. Not in Snow Hill with her parents and siblings, Jessie chose to be in Parksley forever.

2.7

Jessie's Gift

Not love, but loss flooded Jessie throughout her childhood and early adult life. Her mother was cold and distant, worn out, perhaps, by the time the seventh child came along. Her beloved sister, Kate, Jessie's surrogate mother, brushed Jessie's hair, taught her how to skate, ensured that she was impeccably dressed for the class photo. But Kate died when Jessie was not quite thirteen. Older sister Helen stepped into Kate's shoes and was a support to Jessie well into her adult life, but the emotional bond between them was not deep. Jessie adored her father, an imposing figure commanding respect and awe. He was affectionate, but the relationship between them did not compensate for the absence of maternal love. Even if it had, its effect was truncated by his untimely death at fifty-six when Jessie was eighteen.

The deaths of Kate and her father robbed her of love and financial security. The subsequent deaths of her younger brother Jim, Eva's fiancé Robert, and Helen's first husband Eric further contributed to the hardening of a carapace around her which served as protection from pain. But the carapace protected her too well. She developed into a fierce and flawed woman who could not open herself to Empy's love, or mother her daughter with any more tenderness than her mother had mothered her.

Woo at age 93

1985

Jessie's daughter, my mother Helen, also suffered from the paucity of love as she grew up. Empy, whom she adored, was not a strong enough character to fill the emptiness, and Ada, who loved my mother and all the grandchildren, by virtue of her position as a Black maid simply could not fill the void. My mother was the same cold, distant mother to me and my sisters as Jessie had been to her, and her mother, the first Helen, had been to Jessie.

Skipping past my mother to my generation, something magical happened. Jessie was transformed into Woo. She loved me and my sisters unconditionally. She praised me often as I moved through school, then college, and then into a successful career. She never judged me harshly as I had seen her do to others, but was accepting of my choices and decisions. She never chastised me for my divorce, and uttered

Woo's 90th birthday

Left to right on couch: Helen holding Katie, Dick, Woo, Helen, and Marion

Left to right on floor: Amy and Jessie

not a word when Katie came along unexpectedly. When our father refused to support my sister Jessie's desire to get her pilot's license, Woo lent her $10,000. That loan opened the door to Jessie's career as one of the first women commercial airline pilots. Woo also built an affectionate relationship with my sister Marion who, pregnant at the time of Woo's death, was grateful that Woo knew about the impending arrival of another great-grandchild. Sadly, Amy missed Woo's affection because Woo and Empy moved away from Wilmington shortly after their fourth granddaughter was born. She and Amy never got to know each other.

I returned the love that Woo and Papoo bestowed upon me, maintaining close relationships with each of them until their deaths. I also basked in Ada's love for me, and I have no doubt that my liberal attitudes about race in America are infused with her spirit. Additionally, as it became clear that my father would have no sons, and that I was a serious student, he lavished attention on me, the firstborn. I am the one with whom he built a Heathkit radio on which I listened to the Top 40 Countdown throughout high school. I'm the one with whom he built a Van de Graff generator as a science project. Bathed in his pride in my academic achievements, I thrived.

I give full credit to Woo and Papoo for showering me with love throughout my childhood, and I give credit to Ada and my father for reinforcing those early lessons in love. From them all, I learned how to raise Katie lovingly, how to love her father and his children, and now, very late in life, to love a partner who has unexpectedly walked into my life. I am living long enough to watch Katie raise her children in a loving atmosphere and to cultivate a loving marriage with their father. With admiration, I watch my stepchildren transcend, as best they can, the attempts of their mother to establish a regime of bitterness and alienation which, tragically, she continued until her death forty-four years after Dick and I had married.

It could easily have been otherwise. When informed that Dick had fallen in love with me and that we were expecting a child, his ex-wife flew into a torrent of rage and demanded that their children choose between her and him. Despite

Woo and her granddaughters, 1975;
Helen and Jessie left; Marion and Amy right

their joint custody and visitation agreement, she told the children, then ages twelve to seven, "If you go to your father's house, do not come back here." With that pronouncement, she launched decades of pain and trauma that affected us all. Dick and I did not respond in kind, and slowly—ever so slowly—as the children grew up, we built relationships with them grounded in love. At Dick's memorial service and later at the internment of his ashes, we were a family of a grieving widow and five grieving children supporting one another. Although I had given birth to only one of them, they were all my children.

Throughout her life, I noticed Woo's flaws and witnessed her coldness to others. Despite her aloofness to my beloved grandfather, my mother, and my youngest sister, her humiliating behavior at Ada's funeral, and innumerable insufferable episodes in public and private, I always respected and cherished her. As the years have passed, her flaws have melted away. I am now left with overwhelming gratitude for her love—a love which equipped me to end the cycle of loss and lovelessness across generations.

Afterword

In June my sister Marion and I visited the Julia A. Purnell Museum in Snow Hill. The purpose of our trip was to view the portrait of Mary Ann Holland Porter Townsend (1822 -1867) and Jane Holland Townsend Quigg (1835 - 1913) who were cousins and also sisters-in-law. Mary Ann was the mother of James Porter Townsend, Jessie's father, and thus Jessie's paternal grandmother and great-great grandmother to the Brooks girls.

In December, 2023, I sold my house in which the portrait had been hanging. I had moved to a house without an inch of wall space, and I was desperate to find a good home for the portrait. I remembered that the Purnell Museum housed a collection of Uncle Paul's medical instruments (Dr. Paul Jones, brother of Jessie's mother, and a significant influence in Jessie's life). After viewing photos of the portrait and ascertaining that it had an appropriate place to hang it, the museum reported that the portrait would be a welcome addition to the collection. Marion and I left the museum feeling that the Townsend ladies would be well cared for.

Prior to being in my possession, the portrait had hung for decades in the home of our sister Jessie. Prior to that, it had hung in the living room of the Aunts' apartment in Philadelphia where I viewed it with only slightly less trepidation than I viewed the bear by the front door. My grandson Desmond, more decades later, also viewed it with trepidation as he passed "the ladies" on the way to the bathroom in my house. He told me triumphantly one day when he was about four that he wasn't scared of "the ladies" anymore!

We don't know the provenance of the portrait prior to its residence in Philadelphia.

Family lore has it that it was probably painted by an itinerant artist in the 1850's. If that is the case, it was probably commissioned by Alfred James Townsend, husband of Mary Ann, and it probably hung in their home. Perhaps it then passed to their son James Porter Townsend, and his widow, Helen Jones Townsend, took it with her when she went to live with her daughters, the Aunts, in Philadelphia.

Once I made the pilgrimage to Snow Hill to view the portrait, I knew I wanted to preserve it further by including it in *Jessie's Gift*. Jessie and the many generations preceding her all had deep roots in Snow Hill to which her life gave expression and continuity. It is only fitting to include these ancestors in her story.

— Helen Brooks Regan
July, 2025

Family Tree

Appendix 1
Townsend-Lewis-Brooks-Regan Family Tree
James P. Townsend married Helen (1) Jones
1856 - 1910
1858 - 1951
Charles
1880 -1958)
Katherine (Kate)
1881-1905
Helen (2)
1882-1976
Mary
1884-1972
Robley
1885-1886
Eva
1888-1983
James (Jim)
1896-1919
Milton Parks Lewis (Empy) married JESSIE
1898-1962
1892-1987
Richard Brooks married Helen (3)
1913-2005
1917-1995
Richard Regan married HELEN (4)
1938-2019
1945--
Marion
1947--
Jessie
1949--
Mary Amelia (Amy)
1952--
Katherine Helen (5)
1981 --

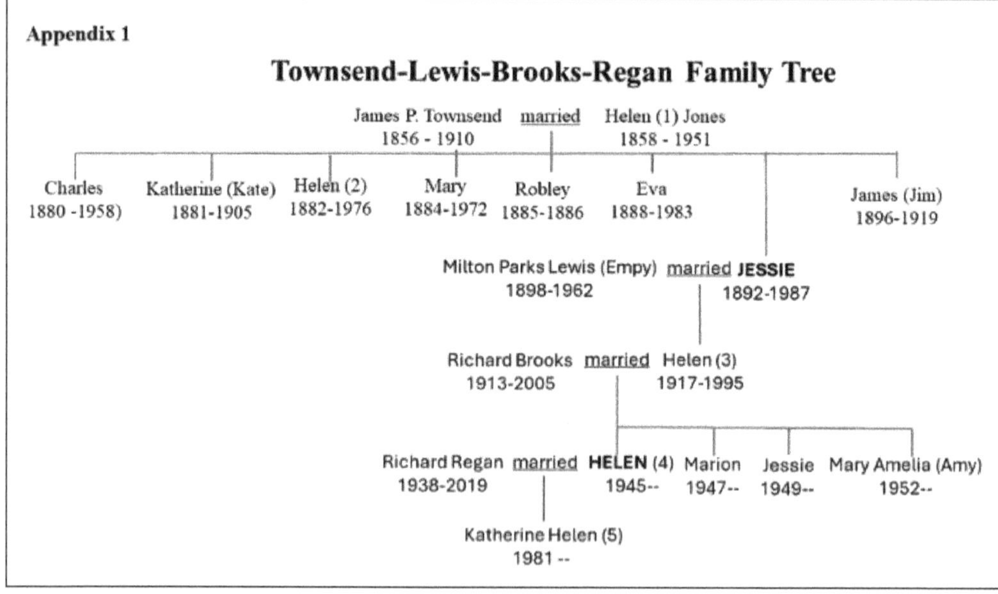

ACKNOWLEDGEMENTS

For about ten years, my writing self has been nourished by a memoir writing group. Initially I was directionless, but with insistent encouragement from its leader, Ann Kimmage, and the supportive critiques of fellow members, I eventually produced a memoir, *A Life Understood.* When I had completed it, I realized to my surprise that Woo had played only a cameo role. This felt like an egregious oversight, and I set out to remedy the situation. As with my first memoir, the writing process itself stimulated many insights into just how significant a role she and Papoo had played in my life, and it enabled me to appreciate more fully the profound significance of Jessie's gift to me.

Over the years, the format of the memoir writing group evolved into a self-directed group with a core membership. These are the women to whom I owe a deep debt of gratitude for *Jessie's Gift*. I doubt that I would have written it without their support and encouragement. Deepest thanks to

Anne Wescott Dodd

Charlotte Fullam

Kay Kavanaugh

Jean Konzal

Eileen Landay

Sue McCulley

Heidi McGinley

Carla Rensenbrink

and to my editor Mary Lib Morgan whose keen eye improved the manuscript considerably.

www.ingramcontent.com/pod-product-compliance
Lightning Source LLC
Chambersburg PA
CBHW041747010726
47507CB00008B/312

* 9 7 8 1 6 2 8 0 6 4 5 5 1 *